The Silent

**Also by Rebecca Kenney**

*Where I Belong*

Rebecca Kenney

The Silent

journey**forth**®

Greenville, South Carolina

**Library of Congress Cataloging-in-Publication Data**

Kenney, Rebecca.
    The silent / Rebecca Kenney.
        p. cm.
    Summary: Seventeen-year-old Nikki has her hands full with being
a high school senior, choosing the right Christian college, and her
parents' failing marriage, but when someone sends threatening emails
to several of her teachers, a police officer asks her to watch and listen
for clues to the sender's identity.
    ISBN 978-1-60682-054-4 (perfect bound pbk. : alk. paper)
    [1. School shootings—Fiction. 2. Interpersonal relations—Fiction. 3.
High schools—Fiction. 4. Schools—Fiction. 5. Christian life—Fiction.
6. Family problems—Fiction. 7. College choice—Fiction.] I. Title.
    PZ7.K3945Sil 2009
    [Fic]—dc22

                                                      2009043259

Design and page layout by Nathan Hutcheon
Cover photo: iStockphoto.com © Simon McConico (person in school
hallway)

ISBN 978–1–60682–054–4

15  14  13  12  11  10  9  8  7  6  5  4  3  2  1

**Publisher's Note**

From its earliest days, JourneyForth has had as its goal to produce books that will increase knowledge and understanding of life and Christian principles and that will help the reader define his response to real-world situations.

*The Silent* uses an all-too-recognizable real-world scenario as the setting for a young Christian's test of faith. While not all will care to read a story of this intensity, many teens will find it relevant and illuminating.

# Contents

1 Dead Zone. . . . . . . . . . . . . . . . . . . . . . . . . . . . . . . 1

2 The Music Begins. . . . . . . . . . . . . . . . . . . . . . 9

3 The Principal . . . . . . . . . . . . . . . . . . . . . . . . . 17

4 Undercover. . . . . . . . . . . . . . . . . . . . . . . . . . . 23

5 Nightmare and Fantasy. . . . . . . . . . . . . . . . . 33

6 Kaye . . . . . . . . . . . . . . . . . . . . . . . . . . . . . . . . 42

7 Bruised. . . . . . . . . . . . . . . . . . . . . . . . . . . . . . 45

8 The Garden of Lost Souls. . . . . . . . . . . . . . . . 53

9 The Source . . . . . . . . . . . . . . . . . . . . . . . . . . . 60

10 Broken Circle . . . . . . . . . . . . . . . . . . . . . . . . . 65

11 Black Water . . . . . . . . . . . . . . . . . . . . . . . . . . 71

12 Taylor . . . . . . . . . . . . . . . . . . . . . . . . . . . . . . . 79

13 Torn Hearts. . . . . . . . . . . . . . . . . . . . . . . . . . . 84

14 Grins and Lies . . . . . . . . . . . . . . . . . . . . . . . . 91

15 Justin. . . . . . . . . . . . . . . . . . . . . . . . . . . . . . . . 99

16 Shadow of Fear. . . . . . . . . . . . . . . . . . . . . . . 105

17 Tears . . . . . . . . . . . . . . . . . . . . . . . . . . . . . . . 111

18 Seeing Blue. . . . . . . . . . . . . . . . . . . . . . . . . . 117

19 Savannah. . . . . . . . . . . . . . . . . . . . . . . . . . . . 125

20 Facing the Music. . . . . . . . . . . . . . . . . . . . . . 131

21 The Silent . . . . . . . . . . . . . . . . . . . . . . . . . . . 139

22 Halloween. . . . . . . . . . . . . . . . . . . . . . . . . . . 141

23 Haley. . . . . . . . . . . . . . . . . . . . . . . . . . . . . . . 148

24 No Eyes Here . . . . . . . . . . . . . . . . . . . . . . . . 152

25 The Myth of the Happy Ending . . . . . . . . . . . 159

# 1

## Dead Zone

---

### Nikki's Digital Diary
<Posted Saturday, October 1, 10:15 p.m.>

I'm Nikki Altemann—seventeen years old and a spy in my own high school.

I don't carry a gun or receive orders through a hidden earpiece.

I carry a book bag, and I do what my parents and teachers tell me to do—most of the time.

But I am a spy. It's my job to listen, and to watch, and to remember. So I'm starting this digital diary on my computer. I'm going to write everything down in this file, even the things that don't seem important—because they might be.

Someone has made threats against my school—against my teachers and my classmates. No one knows who it is, but we have to find out before it's too late.

Before the Silent comes out of hiding.

I'll start at the beginning. For me, the beginning was two days ago on the evening of my birthday.

# The Silent

When my brother opened the kitchen's sliding door at exactly the wrong second, and the wind blew out my birthday candles and splattered wax all over the cake, I knew that the seventeenth year of my life was going to be full of surprises.

Big surprises. The kind that change a person forever.

While I don't believe that humans can know the future, I do believe that sometimes people are allowed to sense a shadow of things to come. And a hurricane-force wind blowing out my candles is definitely a sign of dramatic changes ahead.

"My stars," said my grandmother, waving smoke away from her face. "Shut the door, Taylor!"

My brother tossed his cigarette out onto the wet patio and slid the glass door closed. "Sorry."

I poked at one of the white discs of cooled wax dotting my birthday cake. "You get to pick all these off, Tae."

"I'm sorry, Nikki," said Mom, squeezing my arm. "If Tae hadn't been smoking in the house, this wouldn't have happened."

"And if you could deal with a little essence of tobacco, I wouldn't have had to throw out a good cigarette," said Tae.

"If I hadn't been born, we wouldn't be having this discussion," I said. "I don't know about everybody else, but I want cake."

"Well said!" Dad stepped forward. "I'll slice, and every man can pick the wax off his own piece."

I was about halfway through my piece of cake when my grandmother said, "So Nikki, any more thoughts about college?"

I stabbed my cake. "Not really."

"You're going to have to make a decision soon," said Grandma. "You'll be graduating this spring."

"She has plenty of time," Dad said.

Grandma ignored him. "You know I'll help you out with your school bill if you get into a good university. Unless you're still hung up on attending that Christian school."

"It's a Christian college, Grandma," I said. "And yes, I still want to go there."

Grandma turned to Mom. "Have you talked to her, Julie?"

"I've tried." Mom and Grandma exchanged knowing looks. I felt my face heating up.

"Can we not do this now?" I said. "It's my birthday."

"We're just excited for you, dear." Grandma's thin fingers closed over my arm. "We want you to make the right choice."

"Of course," echoed Mom.

I looked to Dad for help, but he had withdrawn from the conversation and bent his head over his cake. Tae stood by the kitchen door, sucking on his fork and watching the storm. I was on my own.

"You need to have the full college experience, Nikki," Grandma continued. "You need to be exposed to other viewpoints and other kinds of people. And you need a good education—something that a little religious school can't really offer. I'm afraid I can only help with the bill if you choose a college that will really benefit you."

My stomach was tightening up, and I knew that if someone didn't change the subject soon, I was either going to get sick or yell at my grandmother—neither of which would be a very promising finale to my birthday dinner.

"Doesn't she have, like, presents or something to open?" said Taylor, still staring out at the storm.

"Presents? Why, yes," said my mother. "Baby, do you want to open your presents now?"

*My brother, my hero. This time anyway.*

"Yes, I want to open presents!" I said. "Bring 'em on!"

Dad gave me a set of Christian novels that I had mentioned to him, and my grandmother gave me a gift card. I nearly died of shock when I opened Taylor's gift—a poetry book. There has never been anyone less poetic than my brother.

"You like that poem stuff, right?" he said.

"Sure," I said. "Thanks."

And then there was Mom's gift.

The box had wiggly suns and grinning moons all over it. Inside nestled a collection of candles and candle holders, all shapes and sizes. I stared, understanding that the set must have been expensive.

"Wow, Mom," I said. "Thanks! They're beautiful."

"I thought your room needed a little ambiance," she said. "I'll place them for you, if you want."

I knew she wanted to place them where they would facilitate the flow of "chi" or mystical energy or whatever. I avoided looking at Dad; I knew he would be frowning. Again we were on the verge of a family explosion; and, as usual, it was up to me to diffuse the tension.

I reached for the stack of birthday cards from my out-of-state relatives. "Wow, there are a lot of these. I must be more popular than I thought."

Tae snorted. "Don't kid yourself."

Mom slapped his arm. "Be nice. It's her birthday."

I took my time opening each card and reading the sappy greetings inside. By the time I opened the last one, I had a plan for the rest of the evening.

"Anybody want to watch a movie?"

Since I was the birthday girl, I got to pick the movie. I picked a thriller, because anything else would have provoked mockery from my brother and father, and that in turn would have irritated my mom and grandma. But the action kept everyone's attention on the screen, so we made it through the rest of the evening without any major eruptions.

Grandma left for her hotel right after the movie. Tae disappeared to his room.

"Do you want some help carrying those upstairs?" Mom nodded at the presents on the dining room table.

I began piling gifts in my arms. "I think I can manage. Thanks for everything, Mom."

"No problem, Baby. It's your special day." She kissed my cheek. "Sleep well."

By the time I reached my room, her voice had changed, and she was ranting at Dad about something. I kicked the bedroom door closed behind me and dumped my presents on the bed.

I went to the window, opened it wide, and pressed my face against the screen so I could feel the wind and the misting rain. The trees in the backyard swayed, shimmering black and silver against piles of dark cloud. It was the kind of night when strange things could be expected to happen.

Except that nothing ever happened in Mourning, Vermont. Mourning wasn't even big enough to have its own mall; we had to drive nearly an hour to the mall in a nearby town. There were no Christian schools anywhere around, and no churches except for the Kingdom Hall and Saint Mary's and the Methodist church. Every Sunday evening, Dad and I and four or five other families met for worship in the Berkell's living room and listened to a sermon online. Sometimes, when there were enough of us, we even sang a few hymns.

Mr. Berkell said that Mourning was a spiritual "Dead Zone." No one ever talked about God to anyone else unless they were asked. It was just easier not to.

My cell phone buzzed in my pocket. I jumped and pulled it out. The call was from my best friend, Haley Fields.

"Hey, Haley."

"Happy birthday!" Haley shouted in my ear.

"Ow. Thanks."

"Sorry, was that too loud?"

"Just a little," I said.

"I'm sorry I forgot to bring your present to school today! I'll bring it tomorrow, okay?"

"Sure. That's fine."

"What's up? You don't sound birthday-happy."

"My mom and my grandma started on the college thing again tonight," I said.

Haley groaned. "They didn't."

"Did. While we were eating my birthday cake."

"Nikki, I'm so sorry. Where are you?"

"In my room, watching the storm."

"Want to come over?"

5

I sighed. "No, it's late. I should go to bed."

"Well, I'll see you tomorrow."

"Later."

I tucked my phone into my pants pocket and took a deep breath.

"You're going to have to face the music, Nikki," I told myself aloud. I wonder where that term "facing the music" comes from. Music doesn't seem like a very scary thing to face compared to a mom and a grandmother.

No matter how many times I avoid the college topic, eventually I will have to make a final decision. And no matter how I defend my choice, my mother and her mother will object loudly. Do I feel strongly enough about going to a Christian college to deal with that kind of pressure?

A fly looking for a dry spot to rest landed on my window screen. I stared at him, admiring the perfection of his thread-thin legs. I am no fan of bugs—far from it—but the fact that such tiny creatures can function is proof to me that God exists and that He cares about little things. Even though my problems are microscopic compared to, for example, world hunger, I know that He cares.

The next morning I climbed onto the bus, found an empty bench, and plopped my bag down on the seat next to me to save it for Haley. She got on at the next stop and worked her way down the aisle toward me, waving energetically over Randy Wooten's shoulder.

People have asked if Haley and I are twins, which is odd because we're not even sisters, just best friends. I suppose we look sort of alike; we both have light hair and blue eyes, but my hair is caramel colored while Haley's is white blond. She has a round face and dimples, but my face is narrow with high cheekbones. Mom calls them runway cheeks, because they're like the cheekbones of the models you see on TV. If my nose were straighter and my mouth wasn't crooked and my chin didn't have that little cleft in it, I would look like a model. Maybe I can have cosmetic surgery someday.

Haley sat down next to me. "What are you smiling about?"

"Cosmetic surgery."

She stared at me. "Okay. I'm not seeing the funny here."

"I was just thinking about all the things I would have to do to my face to make it perfect."

"It *is* perfect. Perfectly you. Don't be silly."

I grinned. "Thanks."

"I brought your present." Haley pulled a rumpled package out of her bag and handed it to me. "Sorry it's wrinkled. The Porc sat on it at breakfast."

The Porcupine, or the Porc for short, was our nickname for Haley's little brother, whose hair was dark at the roots, bleached at the tips, and stood straight out from his head in a bush of scary spikes. I could see his bristling head several rows up.

The package felt soft, so I figured that the contents had probably survived the Porc's rear without too much damage.

"Open it!" said Haley.

The gift was a black shirt with a pink design of swirls and circles on the front.

"That's the one you liked, right?" said Haley.

"It's the very one." I held up the shirt. "Thanks so much!"

Haley stared past me out the bus window.

"Hey!" I waved my hand in front of her face. "What's up?"

"Police." Haley pointed.

A police car sat in the school parking lot, right next to Principal Rudie's reserved space.

"What are they doing here?" I asked.

"I don't know."

I looked around. By now everyone on the bus had his or her nose mashed against the window; and when the bus pulled up in front of the school, the seats emptied faster than usual.

"Bunch of vultures," I said.

"They're just curious," Haley said. "I'm curious too."

# The Silent

"Probably just a couple of kids doing drugs," I told her.

As I made my way off the bus and along the sidewalk behind Haley, I felt a tug on the strap of my book bag. I turned, and my heart jumped.

"Justin!"

"Hey, Nik. Haley."

As the only Christians at Mourning High School, Justin and Haley and I are close friends. While Haley and I are cute enough to get our own share of attention at school, Justin is the only one of our trio that can be called popular. He has the dark-and-handsome vibe, a sense of humor, and a car. That, for most of the girls at school, is enough to outweigh the Christian factor.

Dad says I'm too young to have a boyfriend, and he is probably right. But when you live in a town as small as ours, with a Christian guy as cute as Justin, it's hard not to develop a crush.

So I took a special delight in the looks that the other girls gave Haley and me as we walked up the steps of Mourning High on either side of Justin.

"What's with the cops?" Justin asked.

"We'll find out eventually," I said. "It'll be all over school by lunchtime."

# 2

## The Music Begins

**Nikki's Digital Diary**

<Continued from Saturday, October 1, 10:15 p.m.>

I underestimated the speed of the gossip network at Mourning High.

---

The minute I sat down in my first class, Maribeth turned around in her seat and said, "Did you hear? Someone sent threatening emails to the teachers this morning. Principal Rudie got one too."

"What kind of threats?"

"I don't know. Something about killing sheeple."

"Sheeple?"

"Yeah, it means people who act like sheep—you know, no will of their own," said Maribeth. "Sheeple just follow along, doing whatever they're told."

"I know what it means," I said. "Who are the sheeple?"

"That's probably what the police are trying to figure out."

"They can trace the emails, right?" I said. "Find out who sent them?"

"Probably."

# The Silent

"Then there's nothing to worry about."

Mrs. Moser walked to the front of the room. "Good morning, class."

It took longer than usual for everyone to settle down and stop talking. In fact Mike and Jamal kept talking and snickering long after the rest of us had quieted. I was surprised when Mrs. Moser did not reprimand them. Usually she did not tolerate chatter in class.

Several times during first period, when the two boys were especially loud, I saw her glance at them. But still she said nothing.

*I wonder if she got one of those threatening emails. Maybe she's afraid.*

In spite of my resolve not to be curious, I found myself wondering exactly what the emails had said, and who had sent them.

To distract myself in the few minutes between Mrs. Moser's class and the next period, I opened the poetry book that Taylor had given me for my birthday. I suspected that it was leftover from the sophomore English class he had taken before he decided that college wasn't worth the money.

The book's pages were mostly crisp and clean, but I found one where the corner had been turned down and then smoothed out again.

I smiled. *Can't fool me, Tae.*

The poem was called "We Wear the Mask" by Paul Laurence Dunbar. What had Tae seen in this poem that made it special enough to mark? I decided to read it.

### "We Wear the Mask"

We wear the mask that grins and lies,
It hides our cheeks and shades our eyes,—
This debt we pay to human guile;
With torn and bleeding hearts we smile,
And mouth with myriad subtleties.

Why should the world be overwise,
In counting all our tears and sighs?
Nay, let them only see us, while
We wear the mask.

We smile, but, O great Christ, our cries
To thee from tortured souls arise.
We sing, but oh the clay is vile
Beneath our feet, and long the mile;
But let the world dream otherwise,
We wear the mask!

The words and the phrasing were old-fashioned, so I did not understand all of it; but it made me shudder.

I looked around at my classmates, chatting and giggling and whispering among themselves. The poem was at least partly true. I knew from personal experience that no one shows their true face—at least not to everyone. I had my school face, my home face, my hanging-out-with-friends face, even my church face. They all looked like me, but they were not all the real me.

What were my classmates hiding under their smiles?

I read the poem again, and then I had to close the book and get out some paper for a quiz.

At lunch I met Justin and Haley in the cafeteria. We sat together at our usual table in the corner. Two of our frequent lunch buddies, Jon Lim and Arisha Khan, were already there.

"We've got to change tables once in a while," I said, setting my tray down. "The other day I heard someone call this the Prayer Table."

Jon grinned. "Not a bad name for it. It's the only table in the place where the food gets blessed."

"That's because we are the only religious freaks in the school," I said.

"That's right," said Arisha. "We freaks have to stick together."

# The Silent

Jon's family is devoutly Buddhist, and Arisha is Muslim. I think they eat with Justin, Haley, and me more out of a desire for acceptance than out of interest in our God.

"So how about those threats?" said Justin after we had given thanks for the food.

Haley shuddered. "It's creepy."

"Does anyone know exactly what the emails said?" I asked.

"'Death to sheeple,'" said Jon. "Five teachers plus the principal got them."

"I heard they said, 'You are all sheeple! I will kill you all,'" said Justin.

"Who did you hear that from?" I asked.

"Tom Hargis."

"Yeah, that sounds like a Tom Authorized Version," I said.

"So who sent it?" Haley asked. "It sounds like a joke, but I guess the police are taking it pretty seriously."

Justin nodded. "They have to."

For the rest of the meal we discussed our weekend plans. Unfortunately mine mostly involved homework, chores, and listening to my parents argue. Correction—listening to my mother argue. Dad has gotten to the point where he just clams up and lets her talk till she is out of breath, which sometimes takes hours. I have learned to tune it out, like when you're sitting in class and the boy next to you has a cold and spends the entire period snorting. You either learn to ignore it, or you go crazy.

I left the lunch table early and stopped by the girls' restroom before class. When I came out, I noticed Carlen Michaels standing by the water fountain.

"Hey, Nikki," she said. "Can I talk to you for a minute?"

Carlen was so gorgeous that you couldn't help staring at her when she passed you in the hall. Her face had smooth Asian lines, but her eyes were bright green. She was part of the A-crowd at Mourning High, one of those people that you never speak to first. I glanced over my shoulder to be sure she wasn't talking to someone behind me.

"Sure, we can talk. What's up?"

She stepped toward me. When she moved, the hair she had arranged over her right eye shifted, and I saw a discoloration around the eye, like a bruise heavily masked with cover-up. But she brushed the hair back into place before I could see for sure.

"Are you okay?" I asked.

"Yeah, sure."

"Do you need the notes from first period? I noticed you were absent."

"Yeah, that would be great."

I shuffled through my notebook. "You can just copy them and give them back to me."

"Okay." She watched me flip through the pages. "You and Justin and Haley are pretty religious, right?"

"We're Christians."

"My friends and I call you three 'The Trinity,' you know, because you're the 'holy kids' and you always hang together."

I frowned. The nickname sounded a little blasphemous to me.

"It's just a joke," said Carlen. "But I'm—I have a problem, and you three are the only religious people I know."

"What do you need?"

"A prayer or two, I guess."

"About what?"

She glanced over her shoulder. The hallway behind her was empty, and for an instant I thought she was going to confide in me. But then she shook her head.

"I can't tell you."

"Then how can I pray for you?"

"You're the religious one. You tell me," she said. "You know what? Forget it. I should have known you couldn't help."

"No, wait!" I caught Carlen's arm. "There is a verse in the Bible that says God knows what we need before we even ask for it. He knows everything; so He'll know what I'm praying for, even though I don't."

"Okay," said Carlen. "Whatever works. Thanks."

She walked away. I stood still in the middle of the hall, convinced that I had handled that situation totally wrong. Carlen was obviously upset, maybe even in serious trouble; she had come to me for help, and I had scared her off.

I thought about the discoloration around her eye. If it was a bruise, that would mean someone had hit her. That meant some kind of abuse, probably by a guy. Her boyfriend maybe? I tried to remember the guys I had seen her with lately; but since she always hung out with groups of friends, it was difficult for an outsider like me to pinpoint any particular boy.

I heard Principal Rudie's voice and turned around. He was coming down the hallway, flanked by our school's safety officer and a blond woman in an immaculate grey suit.

"Not in my school," the principal was saying. "Things like this don't happen in Mourning. It's nothing to worry about—nothing at all. Just some kid looking for kicks, wanting attention. That's all they ever want—attention."

I don't like the principal. He is tall, with thin legs and a beach-ball-shaped belly that juts over his belt. The teachers say he was in the military before he became a school principal, but I figure he must have had an army desk job—or else he has forgotten all his physical fitness training. A trek upstairs to the second floor always leaves him mopping sweat from his forehead. He is constantly looking over his shoulder as if a lawsuit is going to creep up behind him.

"Oh, hello, Nikki," he said when he saw me. "Detective Daulton, this is one of our students. Her father's on the board. Nikki, this is Detective Daulton and Officer Crane."

After quick handshakes all around, they began to move down the hall.

"Principal Rudie?" I stepped forward.

"Yes, Nikki."

"What exactly did those emails say?"

The principal opened his mouth, and then glanced at the detective.

"I'm sorry, Nikki, we're not releasing that information," she said. "I understand your curiosity and your concern. Believe me, we're doing all we can to get to the bottom of this."

I nodded. Of course they were doing all they could.

So why didn't I feel safe?

Maybe it had something to do with the fact that Principal Rudie had not suspended or expelled anyone yet. Did that mean the police didn't know who sent the emails? I'm no computer guru, but I know that emails are usually not hard to trace. If the police couldn't find the sender, then he—or she—must be extra clever.

The warning bell rang, jerking me out of my reverie. The hall instantly filled with students—feet trampling, book bags jostling, voices chattering. I saw Haley and worked my way into the traffic stream beside her.

She glanced at me. "You'll do fine."

"What are you talking about?" I said.

"You look worried," she said. "But it's okay. It's an easy chapter. The questions shouldn't be too bad."

I stared at her, still confused.

"The quiz, silly." Haley laughed.

"Oh. The quiz."

The quiz I had planned to cram for during the last few minutes of the lunch hour.

I wrestled my social studies book out of my bag and began to skim the assigned chapter for important terms and dates.

---

I bombed the quiz. The big negative number at the top of my paper seemed to fit with the rest of this crazy day.

The whole email threat thing still bothers me. There are so many stories on the news about people killing other people for the silliest of reasons. "Sheeple will die." What if the person who sent that really means it? What if he or she is planning something?

# The Silent

"We're doing all we can to get to the bottom of this." That's what the detective said.

But I think she is worried too.

# 3

## The Principal

### In the office of Principal Malcolm Rudie, Mourning High School

Principal Malcolm Rudie was having a very bad Friday.

His wife was out of town visiting her sister, and whenever she was away, he found it especially hard to get up and go to work. He had hit his alarm's snooze button one too many times that morning; and by the time he made it to the school, with his skin still uncomfortably damp under his crumpled blue dress shirt, three teachers were already waiting outside his office.

"Morning, everyone, morning," he said, unlocking the office door. The scent of coffee from the teacher's lounge across the hall made him dizzy. "I'll be right with you, as soon as I get my cup of—"

Mrs. Moser stepped into his personal space and glared at him from behind her black-rimmed glasses. "This can't wait, Rudie. It's important."

"Someone is threatening the school," said Mr. Kepler.

"Threatening the school?" repeated Principal Rudie.

Images of lawyers and courtrooms swam before his eyes, and he heard a flushing sound, like money being sucked down a drain.

"Who's suing us?"

"Not a lawsuit, Rudie." Mrs. Moser spoke as if she were addressing a very small, very stupid child. "Threats."

He frowned at her, not understanding.

"Check your email," said Mrs. Moser. "I'll bet you got one too."

*One of what?* wondered the principal. He opened the office door and entered, the teachers trooping in behind him. Mrs. Mawley and Mr. Kepler sat in the two chairs in front of his desk. Mrs. Moser stood.

Principal Rudie could feel them staring at him. He typed his password wrong twice before finally logging into his computer. The list of unopened emails looked harmless enough.

"Open the one called 'Sheeple,'" said Mrs. Moser.

It looked like a simple spam email until he clicked on it.

When he had read the message, he picked up the phone on his desk and called the sheriff's office.

"Hey, Nick! Morning. I think you'd better send someone over here to the school." He cleared his throat. "Just a minor problem— nothing really—"

"Malcolm, when you call me this early, there's a problem," said the sheriff. "I'll send Cal over. Why don't you tell me about it?"

And that was the beginning of a long day of questions, answers, and more questions. Nick not only sent Officer Cal Lehman over, but a detective as well—a woman with choppy blond hair and sea-grey eyes named Kaye Daulton. She made Principal Rudie nervous.

As he drove home that night, one of the questions she had asked him rolled through his mind again and again.

"Have any of the students exhibited anger or aggressive behavior lately?" she had said.

Principal Rudie had frowned. Of course they had. They were teenagers. Someone was always pushing someone else, or sneering at a teacher, or yelling at a classmate, or vandalizing school property

"This is a high school," he told Kaye Daulton. "We see anger and aggression all the time. Most of the time it's harmless—you know, kids dealing with their emotions, acting out."

"But have you noticed anything unusual?"

He had told her no; but as he drove, he raked through his memories of the past couple of weeks, trying to unearth anything out of the ordinary. He pictured student after student, everyone who had been sent to his office. Emily Meadows, Rob Middleton, Mike Euler and Jamal Dice, Carlen Michaels, Vic Fabiano, Mike Euler again—and on and on it went. He had no idea if any of them had a special tendency to violence or a rage so deep that it might one day express itself in blood.

He parked in the driveway of the townhouse where he and his wife lived. Everest, their Golden Retriever, greeted him from the backyard and kept barking until Principal Rudie unfastened his chain and let him in through the sliding glass door.

"Hungry?" said Rudie to the dog. "So am I."

He poured kibbles into one dish and water into the other, and set both by the back door. Then he hacked a chunk out of one of his wife's frozen casseroles and put it the microwave to heat.

"It's been a long day, Everest," he said. "A long day."

If Trish were here, she would listen to his story while she cooked. She was always interested in his day, whether or not he had anything exciting to report. It annoyed him that she was gone today, when he actually had news. Maybe he would call her later.

Ten minutes later he had settled in front of the TV to enjoy the casserole and watch his favorite crime show. He prided himself on being able to watch without cringing while the medical examiner opened a corpse and searched for the cause of death. But tonight the gunshots in the opening scene shook him up so badly that he could barely hold his fork steady. In the scene the murderer had his head covered with a hood, and Principal Rudie found himself projecting the faces of different students onto that shadowy head.

He shuddered. Suddenly he was triply glad that it was Friday, and that it would be two whole days before he would have to see any of those faces again.

*You're going to have another Columbine right here in Mourning,* he thought.

Ridiculous. The sheriff had a detective on the case. They would find who sent those emails and charge him with something serious enough to teach him a lesson.

Principal Rudie muted the TV and pulled out his cell phone. Detective Kaye Daulton had given him her number in case he had questions or thought of something relevant to the investigation. Well, he had a few questions.

He waited while the phone rang. And rang again.

"Hello, Mr. Rudie," said Kaye's voice. He thought it sounded as chilly as her eyes.

"Ms. Daulton. Sorry to bother you, but I was wondering if you had made any progress."

"Progress?"

"You know, the investigation into the threats on the school. Any suspects yet?"

"Mr. Rudie, we just spoke this morning. I really don't have any more information for you yet."

"I thought perhaps you might have traced the emails or—"

"This is going to take time, Mr. Rudie. We are pursuing a couple of leads right now, and I'll let you know if they yield anything conclusive."

She was giving him official-speak. He cleared his throat, annoyed. "Well then, I'll speak to you tomorrow."

"I'll be sure to give you a call."

"Thanks. Good night."

He pressed the "End" button and tossed his cell phone on the couch. Everest raised his head and sniffed it, then glanced up at Principal Rudie with knowing eyes.

*Something is bothering you,* he seemed to say. *Wish I could help.*

The principal reached down and scratched the dog's ears, trying to ignore the panicky voice in his mind.

*It's going to happen. Right under your nose. You can't stop it.*

Principal Rudie changed TV channels and turned the sound back on. But it didn't help. The voice still chattered and worried in his head.

He stood up, leaving the TV on, and walked through the kitchen to the back door. The glass door was open, leaving only the screen between him and the crisp evening air. The sloping lawn behind the row of townhouses sported a few young trees, the earmarks of a new development. Someday, generations from now, those trees would be thick and tall with leafy crowns just right for shading children at play. That is, unless someone decided to knock down the townhouses and build something else.

A breeze swept toward him, ruffling the grass, and the principal's nose twitched. He smelled something foul, very close to him.

He looked down, and his heart jumped.

On the patio, not four feet away, lay the carcass of what had once been a cat. The principal was about to call Everest and confront him with the crime when he noticed that the cat's body had been flattened, not torn.

He opened the screen door and stepped out. The cat was definitely not dog-kill, but roadkill, a few days old. He could not remember seeing it when he let Everest into the house, which meant that someone had taken the cat's body and brought it here to his patio within the last hour.

His head jerked up, and he eyed the row of backyards and the hedge bordering them. Beyond the hedge lay more backyards and more homes. Anyone could have brought the cat here. Anyone at all.

He told himself that it was just a coincidence—the threatening emails and the dead cat on the same day. Surely nothing he needed to bother the police about. What could they learn from a dead cat anyway?

A smooth golden nose poked over his arm and sniffed the cat. "No, Everest." He pushed the dog away. "Come on, in the house."

Everest stared mournfully from behind the screen as the principal, armed with gloves and a shovel, maneuvered the cat carcass into a black garbage bag. He carried the bag through the house and put it in the garbage can in the garage. He stowed the shovel and gloves before going back inside.

"Well, that's done," he told Everest.

The truck would come for the garbage tomorrow, and he could forget all about the dead cat. The person who put it on the patio was probably hoping for a reaction.

"Sorry to disappoint you," he said to the darkness outside his window. "I'm not so easy to scare."

But he was.

When his wife called, he told her about the threats, but not about the cat. He told himself that he wasn't trying to hide it; it just wasn't important.

He usually made Everest sleep in the kitchen, or even outside, but tonight he stood at the top of the steps and said, "Come on. Come on, boy!" until the dog realized that he meant it and loped up the stairs. The principal put a fluffy towel on the floor by the bed, and Everest settled into it gratefully.

In the night the principal woke from a terrifying dream. He could remember the skeletal heads and ragged fur and glowing eyes of the cats in his dream, so when something cold and wet touched his bare arm, he yelled.

Shaking, he fumbled with the lamp and switched it on. Everest stood beside the bed, staring at him with puzzled brown eyes.

Principal Rudie realized he was sweating as well as shaking. "Good grief," he muttered, getting out of bed. "I'm a wreck. Why did I ever go into this business?"

He did not go back to bed. Instead, he went downstairs, ate a bowl of ice cream, and watched TV until he fell asleep on the couch.

# 4

## Undercover

### Nikki's Digital Diary

<Posted Saturday, October 1, 11:44 p.m.>

Today I slept in until Mom rapped on my door and slid a to-do list underneath it. For a couple of hours I carried laundry, scrubbed shower tiles, and vacuumed carpet, until the growling of my stomach rivaled the noise of the vacuum.

---

I switched it off. "Mom! I'm going to Soza's for lunch."

Her muffled voice responded from somewhere in the basement, and I assumed by the tone of the voice that I had her permission.

Soza's was only a couple blocks away on the corner of Cotton and Darby. I liked the chili cheese fries and the enormous burgers and the shiny red barstools. When I was little I used to stare up at those stools and wonder if I would ever be big enough to sit on one. Even at seventeen, I still feel proud that I'm tall enough to sit comfortably on a Soza's barstool.

I moved into line and studied the menu panels above the counter even though I already knew them by heart. After a moment I recognized the woman ahead of me—the blond detective from school. She glanced back at me, and I nodded to her.

# The Silent

"You go to Mourning High, don't you?" she asked.

"Yes, ma'am," I said, though the answer was obvious.

"I thought I remembered seeing you there. I'm Kaye Daulton."

"The detective. I remember." I held out my hand. "Nikki Altemann."

She shook my hand, eyeing me as though she were measuring me for something.

"When you get your food, would you mind speaking with me for a moment?" she asked. "I'll be sitting right in that corner booth."

"Okay." I swallowed hard.

"Don't worry; you're not in trouble. I need your help with something."

"Okay," I said again.

She ordered her food and moved on to the soda fountain. When my food was ready, I walked to the corner booth and sat down across from her.

"Thanks for coming over, Nikki," she said, glancing at the cheeseburger on my tray. "Please, eat. I don't want to delay you."

"It's no problem," I said, comparing her neatly pressed pants and blouse to my grungy clothes. Did she have to work on Saturdays?

Kaye was silent until I had said the blessing and taken the first few bites of my cheeseburger. Then she said, "This conversation is unofficial. Off the record."

I smiled. She sounded like a character in a movie. "Okay."

"Here's my problem," said the detective. "I could spend a few days at Mourning High, questioning all the students about the threatening emails that your teachers received. That would be an acceptable way for me to gather information about the sender. Not only would it take a very long time, but I probably wouldn't learn anything valuable."

I could see her point. Whenever a teacher, parent, or other grown-up is around, all the students immediately go into "Adult

Alert Lockdown" until the threat is gone. If Kaye Daulton walked around school in her professional capacity, she would collect several bushels of silence and maybe half an ounce of useful information.

I nodded. "The kids won't want to talk to you."

"You, on the other hand, live there every day. You can blend right among the students because you *are* a student. People will talk around you without even noticing that you're there."

"So I'm invisible." I grinned. "Thanks a lot."

"You know what I mean," she said. "No offense intended."

"You want me to spy for you?"

"Don't call it that."

"Okay. You want me to stay alert and tell you if I see anything weird."

"Much better. We've checked into all the problem students," she said. "The trouble is, the obvious suspect isn't always the right one. Whoever sent those notes could be a Silent."

"Silent?"

"My own personal term for someone who stays under the radar, somebody who escapes notice just by acting normal, while inside they are far from it. They're like a briefcase bomb—harmless on the outside, deadly on the inside."

"So I'm looking for a Silent. Or a briefcase."

"Exactly."

"How do you know I'm not the Silent?" I asked.

"You could be," she said. "But if you are, I'm a really bad judge of character. See, I think you're probably more well-adjusted than any other teen in your school."

I raised an eyebrow. "Thanks, I guess." Meanwhile I was thinking, *How does she know how well-adjusted I am? She's known me for all of three minutes.*

Kaye must have guessed my thoughts. "That's not based on my judgment," she said. "After we met you in the hall yesterday, your principal, Mr. Rudie, told me that you are his best student.

Not necessarily the one with the highest grades—but overall, the best."

I was shocked. It was true that I made good grades instead of trouble, volunteered for school events, and tried to be kind and polite to everyone—but best student? Definitely not. The principal must be even more disconnected than I thought. Still, I decided not to call him Roly-Poly Rudie any more, not even in my thoughts.

"I don't know that I would call myself the best student," I said.

"Well, I asked him to recommend a trustworthy source among his students—someone who would be tactful and truthful—and you were his top pick. Don't worry. I did a little research on you before taking his word for it."

"You background-checked me?"

"I just confirmed to myself that you're really the upstanding citizen Principal Rudie claimed you were. It was a necessary precaution; I'm taking a chance here, asking for your help."

"All right," I said. "I'll help you."

"No what's-in-it-for-me line?" asked Kaye, smiling.

"What's in it for me is my safety and the safety of the other students," I said.

"A good way to look at it." She took a card from her purse. "Call my cell if you need me. And give me your number so I'll know who it is that's calling."

I gave her the number, then picked up my tray. "I should go before any of my classmates see us together."

She nodded. "Just listen and look; don't try to dig too much. A vague question or two, maybe; but be careful. A student angry enough to threaten something like this could snap if he's pushed too hard."

I found my own table and settled in with a book and the rest of my meal. A few seconds later, Kaye Daulton left the restaurant. Our meeting at Soza's, at the exact same time on a Saturday afternoon, seemed so convenient that I wondered if she had somehow arranged it. Like maybe she had been watching me. The thought sent a shiver down my spine.

The door opened, and three junior boys from Mourning High entered the restaurant. I hunched over my book and hoped that they wouldn't ask to sit with me. The younger boys at Mourning High had a habit of hitting on senior girls.

Then I realized that eating with them could be the perfect opportunity to begin my investigation into the email sender, the Silent. All I had to do was stifle my inner hermit and bring out my charming side.

I stuffed the book into my bag and watched the boys until I caught Ray Veres's eye. I smiled and waved, and he waved back, flashing me a broad grin. When they had gotten their trays, all three of them headed for my table.

"Hey, your holiness! Mind if we join you?" said Ray, sliding his tray onto the table across from me.

The nickname should have offended me, but his smile told me that he wasn't trying to be cruel. Ray Veres had confused name-calling with flirting since second grade. Maybe someday he would make the transition from rude names to flattering ones.

"Have a seat," I told him. "What's up?"

"Trouble, as usual," he said. "Will's girlfriend just broke up with him."

"That's rough," I said.

"She texted me," said Will. "How lame is that? Didn't even tell me to my face." He let out a string of curse words.

I winced.

"Hey, Will, none of that language around Nikki," said Ray.

"Sorry," said Will. "I'm just really ticked off."

"Let's talk about something else then," I said. "Class, work, those creepy threats at school—"

"Yeah, that's messed up," said the third boy, Cole.

"Who do you guys think it is?" I asked.

Ray shrugged. "Somebody with a lot of anger."

"Somebody messed up," said Cole.

# The Silent

"My girlfriend," said Will.

Ray punched his shoulder. "Get over her, man. She's not worth it. Tell him, Nikki."

"I don't know her," I said. "But I do think it's pretty low to break up with someone by text message."

"Let's drink to that." Ray lifted his cup, and the other boys followed. And because it was only soda, I touched my cup with theirs.

---

## Nikki's Digital Diary
<Posted Monday, October 3, 9:35 p.m.>

Usually my morning bus trip to school consists of a quick mental review of my schedule for the day and a few minutes' chat with Haley. But this morning I actually looked at the kids on the bus . . .

---

I didn't know who I was looking for, and I didn't have much hope that a sudden "vibe" or a shiver down my spine would tell me who the Silent was. I just started with the girls sitting directly in front of me and worked my way forward, looking for anything odd. It was like pretending to be Sherlock Holmes.

I noticed that Stef Rathers had put a blue hoop earring in her left ear and a green dangly one in her right. I noticed that Nina Sherron's sweater was the same one she had worn last fall . . . and the fall before that, only more worn; in fact, there was a small hole on the shoulder seam. Then I noticed how sharp the outline of her shoulder was. Her father had lost his job several months ago; maybe she wasn't getting much to eat. The thought disturbed me.

I looked past Nina. I could put first names with all of the faces, and last names with most of them. Eric Frese, with his greasy hair and ear studs; Drew and Michelle, entwined as usual; Luke Larabee, the tallest guy in school; and the Harpster triplets.

The bus stopped, and Haley got on. I scooted over to make room for her, turning my back to the window so I could see the back rows of the bus out of the corner of my left eye. Will, the boy whose girlfriend broke up with him, was sitting next to a pale guy with vacant blue eyes who reminded me of Peter Parker, Spiderman's mild alter ego. Only his name isn't Peter Parker—it's Todd Kendall, and he's in my afternoon social studies class with Mrs. Mawley.

At the very back of the bus sprawled several black-clad figures jingling with chains and spiky jewelry. All of them wore dark eye makeup—even the boys. They were the "Weird Kids." Justin and Haley and I were weird, in a way, because we were Christians. These kids were weird because they wanted to be. They tried so hard to be different that it was painful to watch. After school they usually hung around the convenience store across the street, sharing cigarettes and music files.

One of the girls caught me watching and stared back. Her hair was dyed black with pink highlights. Her long legs, sheathed in leather lace-up boots, jutted into the bus aisle. She didn't seem offended that I was staring. Instead she smiled at me and nodded. I was so surprised that I almost forgot to nod back; but I did, just before Haley poked me.

"Who are you staring at?" she said. "Do you know that girl?"

I shook my head.

"She looks like a pink tiger," muttered Haley.

Usually I would have laughed with her, but something in me leaped to defend the pink-haired girl. "Be nice," I told Haley.

She raised an eyebrow. "Someone's a grouchy-pants."

"Yeah, well—I've got stuff on my mind." I turned to stare out the window, thinking about the pink-haired girl and her unexpected smile.

How many times did I assume something about a person based only on what I could see—the outside of them? And if the outside was just a mask, how could anyone ever really know anyone else? According to Detective Daulton, there were people in the world who spent months, even years, hiding their true selves until one day the real person burst out.

# The Silent

I kept my eyes and ears open all day. At first I heard nothing that would connect to the threats—just the usual small talk, interspersed with foul words that I tried to tune out. I have decided that my generation must be among the most foul-mouthed in the past couple of centuries. Mourning High School has rules against strong language, of course, but no one ever gets punished for it because the students never curse in the teachers' hearing. And the teachers themselves aren't models of pure speech either.

Mixed in with all the typical talk about homework and crushes and new technology and the unreasonableness of parents, I began to hear other things. It was like listening to an orchestra playing a cheerful marching tune, but with subtle, sinister themes underneath the melody.

"There's a lot of pain in this school," I said to Haley as we stepped out of the front door and headed for the bus. "Like Mr. Kepler in class today, going off on that rabbit trail about betrayal in relationships. That wasn't just a lecture. He was really passionate about it. Like he experienced it personally."

"Maybe." Haley tilted her head to one side. "You've been very mopey all day, Nikki."

"Not mopey," I said. "I've actually been paying attention to other people for a change. It's kind of sad, you know—how we stay in our own little grooves and ignore everyone else."

"Yeah, it really is," said Haley. "But it's so hard, you know? Breaking out of a nice comfy groove."

She snuggled into the bus seat, a smug smile on her face. I laughed and felt better. School was over for the day, and for the next twelve hours I didn't have to think about anyone's burdens but my own.

But I couldn't help being curious about *The Mystery of the Threatening Emails*. (I called it that in my head. It made the whole situation seem less scary and more manageable.) So after dinner, I called Detective Daulton.

"I'm sorry to disturb you," I said. "But if I'm going to help you with this case, I need some more details."

"Like what?"

"Like why haven't you just traced the sender of that original email? Can't you figure out which computer it was sent from?"

"We did. It was sent from a public computer at the Mourning Central Library."

"That's good, right? I mean, don't people have to log in to use those machines?"

"Yes," said Kaye. "And we checked to see who was logged in at the time the message was sent. Unfortunately, that didn't help us much."

"Why not?"

"The user was Mr. Bob Antrell, the pharmacist. He took his granddaughter to the library the previous afternoon and let her use his login for the computer."

"Maybe the granddaughter sent the emails."

"I don't think so. She's six."

"Oh."

"A login session on a library computer lasts for one hour. Mr. Antrell says that his granddaughter only used the computer for half an hour. But neither of them logged out of his account when they left."

"So someone used the computer after him from his account?"

"Yes."

"Which means you can't find out who it was."

"That's right," said Kaye. "The sender used Mr. Antrell's session to open a brand new email account with the username 'Someone1357.' The threatening messages were sent from that account, time-delayed to arrive in each teacher's inbox at exactly 7:30 a.m."

"What about fingerprints? From the keyboard?"

"Impossible to get a clear print," said Kay. "Dozens of people use that computer station, especially during the school year. And we cannot take fingerprints from all the students in the school. We need a suspect."

# The Silent

"I'm sorry if these are dumb questions," I said. "I'm sure you already thought of all this."

"Never be afraid to ask me about anything," said Kaye. "You just might come up with an angle we haven't considered. Unlikely . . . but possible."

# 5

## Nightmare & Fantasy

### Nikki's Digital Diary
<Posted Tuesday, October 4, 11:23 p.m.>

During free period today, I went down to the gym to watch the boys shoot baskets. Maybe guys who work out their surplus energy playing sports are less likely to threaten their classmates, and maybe not. Either way, I have determined that no one will be off-limits in my investigation—no one except Haley and Justin.

---

Justin isn't on the basketball team, but he often joins pick-up games and does pretty well. Today he was on the court with the others.

"Tell me again. Why are we spending free period in the gym?" asked Haley, plopping down next to me on the bleachers.

I shrugged. "Change of scenery?"

She rolled her eyes. "You want to watch Justin. Admit it."

"Okay, you win," I said. It was true. I did want to watch Justin. But I mostly wanted to observe the other guys.

"I hate basketball," said Haley. "The stuffy gym, the sweat, the squeaky shoes . . ."

"The cute guys?" I asked.

"No." She grinned. "Those I don't mind."

Watching those guys work the ball made me thirsty. When I couldn't stand it any longer, I went down to the water fountain in the hall right outside the boys' locker room.

While I was drinking, Luke Larabee came from the gym into the hall, carrying a basketball under one arm. He is six-five and over two hundred pounds, but he has a smile that can melt the hearts of babies, old ladies, and everyone in between.

I backed away from the water fountain, wiping my mouth.

"Hey," he said. "It's Nikki, right?"

I nodded, pleased that he knew my name.

He bent over the fountain and drank.

"You guys are good," I told him.

He shrugged. "Just messing around. But thanks."

I turned to go, but something made me turn back. "Hey, Luke? Do you know anyone who might have written those threatening emails—the ones the teachers got?"

Luke choked and straightened, brushing water from his chin with a hand as big as my head. He towered over me, frowning. "You askin' me that cause I'm black? You think I had something to do with it?"

"No," I squeaked. "I'm asking you because I thought . . . well, I thought you were less intimidating than the other basketball guys. Guess I was wrong."

The frown faded, and he smiled, his teeth brilliant in contrast with his dark skin. I felt like saying, "What beautiful white teeth you have," but I decided against that for two reasons: one, it sounded like something Red Riding Hood might say to the Wolf, alias Grandma; and two, Luke might have thought the compliment had racial undertones.

"Aw, I'm sorry, girl," he said. "I kind of bit your head off there."

"It's okay," I said. "We're all a little tense."

"So what are you doing?" he said. "Trying to figure out who sent those emails?"

"Yes."

"Why?"

"Because I want to find out who's threatening our school."

"Probably just a kid looking for attention," he said. I admired the way his dark, strong fingers closed around the basketball. He flipped it expertly onto the end of his finger and twirled it.

"You're not worried?"

"That someone will come in and shoot us all up? There's a chance of that happening in any school. Way I see it, there's a lesser chance of it here, 'cause we all know each other."

"It just takes one wacko," I said.

"I guess so." He sighed. "You see all this stuff on the news about people shooting their families, shooting strangers. I just keep thinking, maybe if we all took the time to care about each other a little more, stuff like that wouldn't happen. You know?"

"Yeah," I said. "I know."

We walked toward the gym doors.

"I don't know anyone who would have sent those emails," he said. "The guys I hang out with, we're like brothers. If I were investigating—"

"Not investigating," I said. "Curious."

He grinned. "If I were *curious*, I would talk to those geek dudes that hang out with Rob."

"Thanks," I said.

"No problem." He held the door for me, then ran back onto the court to rejoin the game.

When I reached my spot in the bleachers, Haley was smirking at me.

"Well?" she said.

"Well, what?"

"Luke Larabee. He held the door for you."

"So? He's a gentleman."

"Okay then." She looked disappointed, but I was in no mood to talk about boys. I kept thinking about what Luke had said—that I should talk to *those geek dudes that hang out with Rob.*

# The Silent

Rob calls himself "the Source," because Robert Middleton is much too plain a title for someone who knows everything about everyone and every object, not just at Mourning High, but in the whole town and possibly the world. Rob is always connected, always online or on the phone. And everyone knows where to find him. He and his fellow "Info Addicts" hang out on the benches in the hallway between the library and the media room.

There was no putting it off. Sooner or later I would have to talk to Rob—a.k.a. the Source. It might as well be now.

I leaped up from the bleachers. "I've got to go. See you in class."

"What is up with you?" Haley said.

"Sorry," I called over my shoulder. "Catch you later, 'kay?"

I felt terrible, abandoning her like that, but I had only a few minutes to speak with the Source before free period ended.

Rob had his Bluetooth headset in one ear, an iPod earbud in the other, and a laptop balanced on his knee, but somehow he still heard my footsteps and looked up.

"Nicole Winter Altemann," he said, his grin making his chubby face even wider. "What can the Source do for you?"

I didn't ask how he knew my full name. Maybe he meant to impress me, but in a small school like ours, it isn't that hard to discover a student's full name.

"Hey, Robert Mulligan Middleton," I said, tucking my book bag into my lap as I squeezed into the six-inch space on the bench beside him. The Info Addict I had displaced grunted and glared, but I ignored him. I needed the Source's full attention.

"Whatcha need, girl?" said Rob.

"Information."

"Who doesn't?" His grin widened. "What, specifically?"

I looked around at the five geeks of various shapes and sizes huddled around us. There was no point in trying to get Rob alone to ask him anything. He would only turn around and tell his pals anyway.

"I'm curious about those threatening emails," I said. "The ones that were sent last week. Do you know anything about that?"

Rob's grin vanished. "You mean, did one of us send them?"

I shrugged. "Or can you find out who did?"

"What's it to you?" said Rob. "The dude who did it was probably harmless, just trying to feel important, you know? Shake people up a little."

"But what if it's more than that?" I asked. "Aren't you scared?"

Rob shook his head. "I don't know anything about it. The police already asked me a bunch of questions."

"Yeah, you and your pals are probably top on their list of suspects," I said.

"Okay, look," he said. "I don't know why you're so curious, but I'll tell you what I told the police. I think there *is* somebody at the school who is planning something. None of us—" he nodded to his friends—"know what or when or who. But there are bad vibes."

"Vibes?" I said. "I thought you guys dealt in logic and hard facts. Zeros and ones, to be exact." I grinned at the surprise on their faces. "What? A girl can't know binary?"

Rob laughed.

"It's more than a vibe," said Micah, a skinny Info Addict with a long nose and unnaturally bright blue eyes. "Weird stuff goes on in people's heads. Guys write on the stalls in the bathrooms, and I've seen some pretty scary things."

"You probably wrote most of them," murmured one of the other boys, and Rob laughed again.

Micah glared at the other boy and continued. "Not raunchy stuff—stuff about killing and death and shooting people in the head and masks."

"Masks?"

"Yeah. The mask stuff is in the bathroom by the library."

"Can you show me?"

He stared at me as if I had suddenly gone mad. "It's a dude's bathroom, Nikki!"

"Oh, right. Okay, can you tell me any more details?"

"Not really. It's just a few words and pictures."

"Did you show them to the police?"

"No."

"Why not?"

Micah shrugged. "It didn't seem important."

I jumped up, and the guy on the end of the bench tumbled off with a yelp. "Thanks, guys. Email me if you think of anything else."

I walked away, knowing I would receive at least four or five emails by the end of the day. Most of the geek guys were friendly, and all of them were smart, but only a few had girlfriends. They would take any excuse to dialogue with a girl. And maybe in the process I would glean some more information.

In the meantime I needed to find out more about the *mask stuff* Micah had mentioned. I considered getting one of the boys to draw me copies of the suspicious pictures. I even began practicing the conversation in my head.

I would find one of the boys in the hall. "Hey Todd. You like to draw, right? Could you do me a really big favor?"

I would smile, maybe bat my eyelashes a few times.

And of course he would say, "Sure, Nikki, whatever you want."

"Could you go in the guys' bathroom and copy down all the words and pictures you see in the stalls and give them to me?"

No way was I ever having that conversation. I would die first.

Of course that only left me one other option, only a little less horrifying than the first. I would have to pay a visit to the most disgusting place in the universe—a high school boys' bathroom. I needed to see the pictures Micah had mentioned. And I had to do it without getting caught by students or teachers.

The answer, of course, was to go in the bathroom in the evening, when the janitorial staff was cleaning. Unlike most of the students at Mourning High, I knew the woman who cleaned the restrooms, Jeanine Howell. Maybe I could bribe Mrs. Howell to let me sneak a peek into the boys' restroom.

When I got home after school, I raided the pantry. Mom always kept a bag of chocolate chips in there, in case of a "cookie emergency." I decided that my investigation qualified for emergency cookies. Fortunately for me, Mom would not be home till late, so I could do what I wanted in the kitchen.

Much flour and grease and several burns later, I had three dozen bribe-worthy cookies and two dozen crooked or dark ones that our family could eat.

Now, to get myself and the cookies to school. I didn't relish the thought of riding my bike all the way there while at the same time trying to balance a container of cookies. But neither Mom or Dad were home, so borrowing one of their cars was out of the question.

I was about to pick up the phone and ask Haley about her mom's car, when Tae clumped into the kitchen, grabbed three cookies, and said, "I'm going out. Be back later."

"Hey, can I come with you?" I asked.

He frowned.

"I don't mean to hang out. It's just that I have to deliver some of these cookies to somebody at school, and I don't want to juggle them on my bike."

He chewed slowly, staring at me. Then he took another bite, which for him was half a cookie, and chewed that slowly too. I knew he was only doing it to annoy me, so I pretended to wait patiently.

"Hmm," he said at last. "I suppose I could drop you off there. But how are you going to get home?"

"We could stick my bike on your rack. I'll ride back later."

"More work," he said. "I'm not a fan of work."

When I still didn't engage, he sighed. "You're no fun tonight, Nik."

"That's because I'm in a serious mood. See? This is my serious face."

# The Silent

"All right. Come on."

He dropped me, my bike, and the cookies off in front of the school. I went to the side door nearest the dumpster, the one that the janitorial staff always prop open while they're cleaning. I don't know if they're supposed to leave it open, since anyone could walk in, but they do it anyway.

I had been in the school when it was empty, but only a few times, and always with an adult. I walked through the halls until I saw Mrs. Howell's cleaning cart by the library bathrooms. I took a deep breath and gripped my container of cookies. This was going to be an awkward conversation.

As I approached the boys' bathroom door, I heard music . . . and singing. Deep, throaty, enthusiastic singing. Mrs. Howell was in the bathroom with a radio, singing along while she cleaned.

I tapped on the door, softly at first, then louder. Mrs. Howell just kept singing, so at last I pushed open the door and stepped in.

"Mrs. Howell?"

She yelped and nearly squirted cleaner in my face.

"It's just me," I said, trying not to laugh. "Nikki Altemann. I brought you some cookies."

"Cookies, eh?" she said. "What do you want?"

I didn't even try to pretend that they weren't a bribe. "I'd like to look around in here. I need to see something that someone wrote in one of the stalls."

She squinted at me. "Some teen crush thing, eh? Your crush wrote some other girl's initials on the stall instead of yours."

I squirmed. So far I wasn't breaking any rules, and I didn't want to taint my investigation with a lie.

Apparently the squirming was enough of an answer for Mrs. Howell. "Go on," she said. "Take a look. But don't touch anything, and be quick. You've got three minutes."

She checked her watch, and I knew she wasn't kidding. She was taking a risk, letting me run around the school after hours, trusting me not to steal or sabotage anything.

I set the cookies on the counter, trying not to focus on anything in the bathroom except what I had come there to see. I stepped carefully across the freshly mopped floor to the stalls and opened each one in turn. The drawings Micah had mentioned were in the one farthest from the door. They were small and neat, etched along the lower edge of the stall partition—black stick figures wearing masks, with a larger figure aiming a gun at the head of one of them. They reminded me of cave paintings.

Quickly I opened my phone and snapped a picture of the sketches. Then I ran out of the bathroom and took a deep breath of untainted air. Mrs. Howell was heading my way with her cart.

"Thank you," I said as I passed her.

She nodded. "You found what you were looking for?"

"Yes."

"Well, then, we'll forget all about it."

I smiled at her and hurried out of the building.

During the bike ride home, I thought about those masked figures. Someone was depicting either their nightmare or their fantasy.

So which was it?

# 6

*Kaye*

## At Kaye Daulton's desk, Mourning Police Department

Drawings? In a boys' bathroom?

Kaye didn't know whether to laugh or cry about Nikki's latest bit of "information."

"I admire your dedication," she said. "I'll certainly put this in the file."

She hung up as soon as it was politely possible. Then she propped her elbows on the desk and rested her head in her hands.

Kaye wasn't sure how she felt about recruiting a teenager to be her eyes and ears at Mourning High. Teenagers were unreliable, unpredictable, and prone to bite the hand that tried to help them. Nikki seemed to be more socially aware than most of her peers, but there was no way for Kaye to be sure of that. She had to trust the girl.

That was hard, especially since Kaye could remember exactly how untrustworthy she herself had been at seventeen.

She forced her eyes open and stared at the report on her computer screen. When her vision blurred like this, it was definitely time to go home—or to get her eyes checked again.

She logged out of her machine, stacked some papers together, and stood up.

"Heading out?" said George, looking up from his own pile of paperwork.

"Yeah." Kaye switched off her desk lamp. "You?"

He shook his head. "I have a little more research to do. I'm trying to nail down a couple of names in the Perch area drug case."

Kaye walked over to his desk. "Mind if I look?"

"Go ahead."

That was one thing she liked about George. He was never possessive of his cases. He never wanted glory for himself. If someone else could solve a case quicker than he could, he simply rejoiced that it was solved, rather than getting jealous.

Kaye snagged the corner of a photo in the pile and pulled it out. "Who's this?"

"Casey Wozniak. I think he's some kind of middleman, like maybe he stores the stuff. But I'm not sure."

"Have you searched his place?"

"If I tried to get a warrant with what I have on him right now, they'd refuse it."

"So basically all you've got is your instinct."

"Exactly." He sighed. "But I hope to have more soon. Rita will be watching Casey's house tomorrow night; maybe she can document some drug activity there, something I can show to the judge."

"Well, good luck." She laid the picture back on his desk.

"How about you? Any breaks in that high school case? The email threats?"

Kaye chewed her lip. "Bathroom art."

The look on George's face was priceless. She laughed.

"Do I want to know?" said George.

"Probably," she said. "But I'm not going to tell you."

She saluted him and walked through the office, waving to Stella and Regan on her way out. "Don't work too late," she called to them.

# The Silent

By the time she reached her car, her mood had darkened again. She felt guilty for joking about the Mourning High case with George. A potential teenage killer was nothing to laugh about. There were news stories every day about kids who couldn't handle their problems and decided to solve the world's injustices with a gun and a few rounds of ammo.

Funny how adults often tried to solve things that way too, except they usually had better judgment when identifying the enemy. To a teen with a heart full of agony and a head full of confusion, the enemy was usually someone close to him—parents, neighbors, teachers, classmates. People within his circle.

Nikki's face resurfaced in Kaye's mind. There was something different about her. She was a beautiful girl, but that wasn't it. When you looked in her eyes, she looked back at you. She was *there*. She could listen, and she made people want to confide in her.

Kaye had met the type before, first in her own mother and now in Stella. Stella had the same inviting personality and listening skills, and she used her abilities well as a crisis counselor and negotiator for the Mourning Police Department.

But Nikki wasn't just a good listener. She had standards—a moral code—and that impressed Kaye. Not everyone believed in right and wrong anymore.

And Nikki hadn't become Kaye's eyes and ears just because she thought it was cool, or because she wanted to play spy, or because she wanted a reward. She had said, *What's in it for me is my safety and the safety of the other students.*

Principal Rudie had mentioned that Nikki was Dave Altemann's daughter, and Kaye knew that Dave was a Christian. Maybe Nikki was too. That would explain the moral center, the sense of personal responsibility.

She thought of asking Nikki about it. But delving into the girl's personal beliefs would go beyond business. It would mean friendship—actually caring about the kid. And Kaye wasn't ready to do that.

And she wasn't ready for belief. Not yet.

# 7

## Bruised

### Nikki's Digital Diary
<Posted Wednesday, October 5, 10:03 p.m.>

I have a new investigative policy—no prying. Since asking questions hasn't gotten me anywhere, except into a stinky restroom with cryptic "stall paintings," I've decided to do what Kaye first asked me to do—listen.

It's amazing what you find out about people when you start listening and looking. You can walk past someone a dozen times a week and never know a thing about them. It takes effort to pull back the curtain . . . to really see.

---

At lunch today I was in line behind Carlen Michaels, and I noticed four oval bruises on her left upper arm. They looked as if they had been left by fingers.

I remembered the bruising around Carlen's eye, and again I wondered if she was being abused. Was that why she wanted prayer? Should I pull her aside and ask her about it? But that would be too awkward. Surely I wasn't the only one who had noticed. She has friends around her all the time; one of them would ask her about it. I didn't have the right to pry.

# The Silent

I kept an eye on Carlen during lunch. She sat with Randy Wooten and two girls. I wondered if Randy might be the one hurting her, but they didn't act like they were dating. In fact, from what I could see, Randy barely spoke to her at all.

Arisha touched my arm. "You okay?"

I turned my attention back to our table. "Sure. Just zoning."

Arisha nodded and went back to her food, but Haley glanced at me as if to say, "Yeah, right. You can fool her, but you can't fool me. Something's going on."

I knew she would expect me to tell her about it later.

I had been so intent on spying on Carlen during lunch that I drank glass after glass of water without noticing. So halfway through my first class of the afternoon, I had to run to the bathroom.

Carlen was standing in front of the mirror when I came in, examining her arm. She turned away when she saw me and disappeared into one of the stalls.

While I was washing my hands, she came out again. The silence was agonizing. I had to say something. But what?

Finally I settled for the time-honored question, "Are you okay?"

She kept lathering her hands with soap. I wondered if she had even heard me. Then I glanced at her face in the mirror, and even though she held her head down, I could see that she was crying.

"Carlen." I tossed my used paper towel in the trash and put my hand on her shoulder. "What's wrong? Is somebody hurting you?"

She lifted her head. Her eyes and nose were red and puffy with trying to hold the tears in.

"It's okay to cry," I said.

She began to sob, her fingers gripping the counter and her shoulders heaving. I patted her shoulder and handed her tissues from the box by the sink.

"Do you need to talk to somebody?" I asked.

Carlen sniffed. "I can't," she said.

"Why not?"

"If he finds out that I told on him, he'll just hurt me again," she said.

"Who?"

She shook her head. "No! I can't tell anyone, okay? Just leave me alone."

"Not a chance. Look, you can trust me."

She pressed a tissue to her left eye, then her right. "Look at me. I'm a mess."

"You're just upset." Again I noticed the bruises on her arm. "Who did that to you, Carlen?"

She sighed. "Doesn't matter."

"Yes, it does. Carlen, you're a human being, not a punching bag. You shouldn't let anyone get away with treating you like this."

"You're sweet, Nikki." She sighed again. "But it's not that simple."

On a hunch, I asked, "Is it Randy?"

Carlen burst into tears again. "How did you know?"

"Just a guess."

"He's usually so kind to me. He treats me like queen most of the time. But he's so jealous! If I talk to another guy, or if I tell him that I need some space, he gets furious and says that I don't love him. He says that if I leave him, he'll hurt himself. And I don't want that."

*This is way over my head*, I thought.

"Carlen, you need to talk to Ms. Benato."

"The counselor? No, I can't. I'd be betraying Randy. He needs me. I just have to learn how to avoid making him so angry."

"Carlen, the best way to help him and yourself is to tell someone. Now, if you don't tell Principal Rudie or Ms. Benato, I'll have to."

She frowned. "Are you threatening me? I thought you said I could trust you!"

"It's not a threat," I said. "But I've heard that people in the middle of a situation like this can't always see clearly. I'm just trying to help you do the right thing."

For a minute I thought she would storm out of the restroom. But instead she nodded. "All right."

I took her arm. "I'll go with you."

We went out into the hall together. I was a little nervous about skipping class, but I figured that Ms. Benato would write an excuse for me.

We were a few doors away from her office when I saw Randy coming toward us. Carlen saw him too. I felt her arm go rigid.

"Hey, baby," he said, ignoring me. "Aren't you supposed to be in class?"

"I was—I—"

"We were just talking," I said.

Randy didn't turn toward me. He kept his eyes locked with Carlen's. "You look like you don't feel well," he said. "Come on. I'll take you home."

"Okay," she whispered, taking her arm from mine. I grabbed it.

"Wait, Carlen. He's just going to hurt you again."

Randy laughed, but there was an edge to the sound that frightened me. "Hurt her? Why would I do that?" He took Carlen's hand and stroked it. "Have you been telling stories, Carly?"

"No." She pulled her arm away from me again. "I would never tell stories about you, Randy."

"Good. Now come on."

His voice was calm, but his face was growing redder by the second. Carlen hesitated.

"Randy, I think I'm going with Nikki."

"No, you're not."

I saw his hands tighten, and Carlen sucked in a quick breath.

"This has gone far enough," I said. I ran to Ms. Benato's office and burst in without knocking.

She rose from her desk at once. "Nikki? Is something wrong?"

I pointed down the hall, where Randy was trying to force a weeping Carlen to come with him.

"I think he's been beating her," I said. "He doesn't want her to talk to you."

Ms. Benato's face hardened, and she strode toward the two of them.

"Randy Wooten!" she said in a thunderous voice. "Let her go now!"

Randy glared at her, but he let go of Carlen.

"Carlen, come with me, please," said Ms. Benato. "Randy, you go to Principal Rudie's office. Now! I'll be there shortly."

I didn't want to be left alone in the hall with Randy, so I followed Carlen and Ms. Benato into the counselor's office and sat there until Ms. Benato gave me a note and sent me to my next class.

By the end of the afternoon, rumors were all over the school, most of them unrecognizable mutations of the truth. Nobody mentioned my part in the story, and I didn't offer any information, not even to Haley.


Dad and I don't usually go to the Wednesday night prayer meeting at the Berkell's, but tonight he came home from work early, so we went. The Berkells live in what Mom calls the "fancy area" of Mourning, in a big grey brick house with an immaculate green lawn. Mr. Berkell met us at the door and shook hands with Dad.

"Dave, great to see you! How's it going?"

"Great," said Dad. "Everything is great. How are you?"

"Busy, but good," said Mr. Berkell.

Dad nodded and started to move into the house, but Mr. Berkell touched his arm.

"How are you and Julie doing?" he asked, and by his tone I could tell he was asking about more than general health and well-being.

"Fine, fine," said Dad. "We're both fine."

*Just say it, Dad. Tell him that you and Mom can't speak to each other without getting into a fight. Tell him that Mom shows zero interest in Christianity.*

# The Silent

But no, he had to pretend that everything was "fine." It must be some kind of male pride thing. Maybe I should take Mr. Berkell aside and explain to him how things really are at home. But it's not my business to tell on my dad. He will have to open up on his own.

Our "church sanctuary" is the Berkells' expansive living room with spotless beige couches and chairs for pews. Mr. Berkell is a software programmer, so he has one of the largest houses in Mourning, complete with the nicest furniture. Whenever we listen to a sermon about covetousness or envy, my eyes always travel to the gigantic TV and audio system in its shiny black cabinet. That and the media collection covering an entire wall of the room are two things that I envy every time I step into that house.

Justin and his parents were already in the living room when we arrived. Dad steered me toward the two vacant seats near them. I felt myself blushing as I sat down on the sofa next to Justin.

"Hey, Nik," he said.

"Hey, Justin."

I spent the next few minutes trying to think of something enchanting to say. *How is your week going?* No, I had seen him every day this week. *Nice weather today, isn't it?* But it wasn't. It was cold, wet, and windy—typical autumn weather in Vermont.

Haley and her mom came in with Haley's little brother Liam— a.k.a. "the Porc"—in tow. When the Porc's eyes met mine, he grinned and stuck out his tongue. I made a horrible face at him and then realized that Mrs. Fields was staring at me.

"Are you okay, Nikki?" she asked, frowning.

"Yes, ma'am," I said. "Just playing around with the Por—with Liam."

Haley's eyes sparkled with suppressed laughter as she found a seat on the opposite side of the living room next to Mrs. Land.

I like Mrs. Land better than Mrs. Berkell. Mrs. Berkell loves God and loves to have all of us meet for church in her house, but when you ask her for advice, she just repeats what I call "Christian catch-phrases" like "When God closes a door, He opens a window" or "God will never give you more than you can handle." Those things are true, I suppose; but if simply quoting them could fix any problem, life would be perfect.

When I want real advice, I talk to Mrs. Land. She's African American and gorgeous. When she was young, during what she calls her "pre-Jesus days," she modeled for magazines.

After the Bible study and prayer time, I pulled Mrs. Land aside.

"What's on your mind, honey?" she asked.

"I've been talking to some people at school," I said. "You know, listening to their problems and all that. And it's making me kind of sad and depressed."

Mrs. Land nodded. "When someone tells you about their pain, you automatically take a share in it. That share is bigger if you're a Christian, or even just a good-hearted person. You're carrying pieces of all the sorrow and pain that your schoolmates have told you about, and it's weighing you down. It's a burden on your heart."

A burden? That sounded like something a depressed mom or a pessimistic old lady would talk about. High school girls like me don't carry *burdens*.

"So how do I get rid of it?" I asked.

Her beautiful smile had a hint of sadness in it. "You don't."

"Why not?"

"The only way to get rid of a burden like that is to stop caring about other people."

"What about helping them?" I asked. "That's an option, right?"

"Of course," said Mrs. Land. "But the more involved you get in a person's life, the more painful it is to you personally when the trouble gets worse. So it really comes down to the Bible principle of loving others more than you love yourself. And that's pretty hard."

"What about a person who really needs help, but doesn't want it?" I asked. "How do you deal with that?"

## The Silent

She sighed. "I haven't figured that out yet, honey. I suppose you can try to help whether they want you to or not, but if their heart isn't in it, there's no way that any good change is going to last. I suppose in that case, the best thing you can do is pray."

---

I know she is right, but prayer is often very trying to my patience. Sometimes I wish God would just step in and force people to do the right thing. And then I take a step back and realize how good He is *not* to do that. He wants us to have a choice. If He forced us all to love Him and do right, what would He have but a world of little robots with no minds of their own? But He wants us to learn and think and choose to love Him.

# 8

## The Garden of Lost Souls

### Nikki's Digital Diary
<Posted Thursday, October 6, 8:50 p.m.>

The situation with Carlen and my conversation with Mrs. Land made for some pretty restless sleep last night, complete with bad dreams featuring Randy. So I'm going to write this entry as quickly as I can and try to get to bed early tonight.

---

This morning before school, I called Kaye and told her about Randy.

"An abusive type," she said. "Definitely someone to keep an eye on. I'll call your principal today and see if I can talk to this kid."

"I've got to go," I told her. "My dad's calling me. Talk to you later."

Dad was yelling from downstairs. "Nikki, the bus is here."

I yelped and snatched my bag. "Coming!"

The bus driver, Mr. Hayes, was pulling away as I ran out, but he stopped when he saw me. I climbed up the steps, conscious that I hadn't straightened my hair or put in earrings.

# The Silent

When Haley sat down beside me, I said, "Do you have any spare earrings?"

"Just a second." She opened her purse and dug in a side pouch with two fingers. "Here."

She dropped the earrings into my hand. They were large, bright pink stars. "I can't wear these!" I said. "I have a red shirt on."

"Sorry, that's all I have. So are you going to have naked ears, or are you going to clash?"

I sighed. "Clash, I guess. Ugh."

As we merged into the crowd of kids in the hall, someone tapped my shoulder.

It was the girl from the parking lot—the one with the pink hair. Up close she looked younger and smaller, in spite of the high heels. She was probably a sophomore, maybe even a freshman, which would explain why I had never seen her in any of my classes.

"Can I talk to you for a second?"

"Sure."

We moved out of the crowd.

"I overheard you asking Rob about those emails—you know, the threats," she said. "If you're trying to figure out who it was, there's something you should check out."

"What?" I asked.

"The Garden of Lost Souls," she said.

I raised an eyebrow. "The garden of what?"

"The Garden of Lost Souls. It's a blogging community. You can get a free blog and post whatever you want. I blog all the time."

"I don't mean to be rude," I said. "But what does this have to do with the emails?"

"All I know is that there's someone else from Mourning High who blogs there. She mentioned it once, a while ago. She calls herself 'TheFourthFate092.'"

I crossed my arms. "Still not seeing how this is relevant."

"Read the blog," she said. "You'll see."

"Okay," I said.

She shifted her weight from one four-inch heel to the other. "I'm Jasmine."

"Nikki."

She nodded, and I nodded back.

"Right," she said. "I'll see you around."

"See you."

I slid into my seat just before the bell rang. Haley stared at me, unsmiling. I knew she was wondering what conversation I could possibly have had with one of the Weird Kids.

After class, she walked silently beside me until I couldn't stand it.

"Okay, what's up with you?" I asked.

"What's up with *me*? You're one to talk."

I stared at her. "What's that supposed to mean?"

"You think I haven't noticed? You're using every spare minute to sneak around school and chat with people you barely know, including that punk girl."

"Don't be catty, Haley," I said. "She's nice."

"Whatever. You may be fooling everyone else, Nikki, but you are not fooling me. You're up to something."

"Maybe."

"And you won't tell me about it?"

"I can't."

She shut her mouth tight and nodded as if to say, "I thought as much."

"Come on, Haley," I said. "I don't want to hide things from you, but in this case I have to. Please don't be mad."

She kept walking without answering. I knew from experience that it would take her a while to cool down and revert to her usual cheerful self. Inwardly I groaned. Here was yet another bit of drama to add to my ever-growing pile.

After finishing my homework this evening, I sat down at my computer and typed "The Garden of Lost Souls" into the search bar. Among the movies, music, and books that surfaced, I found one website that looked promising. I didn't usually visit strange sites, but this was too important to be picky.

# The Silent

When I clicked on the link, a blogging site appeared. Green vines twined around grey pillars against a black background. Even though I already have my own blog, I had to sign up for a free blog on "Garden of Lost Souls" before I could access the user content. Once that was done, I found TheFourthFate092's blog easily.

FourthFate's profile picture was a black and white face, distorted like a reflection in a wavy mirror. It looked like a girl, but it was so skewed that I couldn't tell if I knew the face.

I clicked on her first post.

*I'm seventeen years old. I go to high school in a little town called Mourning where nothing ever happens. And I hate my life. I guess that's why I'm starting this blog. I have to tell someone, or I think I might die.*

*Last summer I went to stay with my dad for vacation, and I met this guy. I thought he was the nicest, cutest person in the world. We had two awesome months together, and then I had to come back to Mourning. He said he would email and call. But he didn't. He never answered one of my emails.*

*I thought he was the one. I thought we were made for each other. He was everything. I feel so drained, so empty. No one cares for me here. Mom is always too busy to talk.*

I skimmed through several more posts in which The Fourth Fate talked about the boy who had broken her heart. I could tell that time was making her depression worse instead of better.

*I thought about him again today. I tried not to, but I couldn't help it. He was such a part of me. We did everything together. Now it's like there's a long, long ravine cutting across the middle of my heart. I keep trying to find something that will fill it—but nothing does.*

*He said that he loved me—it was so easy to believe him.*

*The other day I saw on his Facebook page that he's dating somebody else. The pain is just too much to bear.*

Someone called "Woozifrog" had commented on this section—some kind of fluff about "forgetting the rat that did this to you and loving yourself."

The more I read about TheFourthFate's broken heart, the more thankful I was that my dad was so strict about my dating life. I wouldn't want to endure the kind of pain this girl was going through—not in a hundred million years.

I clicked on the next post.

*No one at school cares. They're like robots. They follow their little preplanned tracks from home to class to another class to lunch, and then to more classes and back home again. Not one of them cares about anyone but himself. I know the other girls think I'm sick, or anorexic, or something. They stare at me all the time because I'm too thin and too pale. Sometimes I just want to hide from them, and sometimes I get so angry that I want to make them all hurt as much as I'm hurting.*

"Nikki!"

I jumped. "Yes, Mom?"

"Nikki, could you help me with something?"

"Sure." The moment I closed the browser, the room seemed to brighten. The cloud of FourthFate's pain was gone, but a shadow of it stayed in my thoughts as I went out into the hall.

Mom was lugging black plastic trash bags out of her room. "Give me a hand with these, hon," she said.

I picked up two, noticing that the tops were secured with little white twist ties. "What's in here?"

"Oh, just some stuff I'm giving or throwing away," she said.

I helped her load the bags into her car. "Want me to come along and help you unload it?"

"No, that's all right," she said. "The charity people will help me. You run along back to your game or whatever."

I went back inside. When I reached my room, I heard Mom's car pulling out of the driveway and glanced outside. She was turning right out of our driveway, the opposite way she should be going to reach the donation center. Maybe she had an errand to run first.

I did not feel like reading any more of FourthFate's depressing blog posts, so I flopped down on my bed to think.

FourthFate offered few clues about her personal life. I pulled a notebook from my bag and made a list of all the things I knew about her.

Female
Attends Mourning High
Parents divorced
Dad lives in another city
Visited dad last summer
Is thin and pale
Has a Facebook page

I leaned back against my pillows and sighed. Those seven clues described at least a dozen girls at Mourning High—probably more.

I got up and combed through the blog posts again, scrutinizing every sentence. FourthFate's posts were always short and more full of inner pain than actual details. I suppose that was a good idea; if you're going to post your bleeding heart online for everyone to see, you should maintain anonymity as much as possible. But it didn't help me in my quest to find out who she was.

"Who are you, FourthFate?" I said to the computer screen. "Give me a hint."

I hit the "back" button to return to FourthFate's main page. For a minute I couldn't believe my eyes.

A new blog entry had appeared—posted one minute ago.

"Okay, this is creepy," I whispered.

I clicked on it.

*I don't feel like doing anything. What's the point? I don't care about homework, or grades, or class, or anything. I lie on my bed and watch TV. I hate myself for being such a loser, but I'm just not interested in life. It's just one big monotonous circle, and I want out.*

*Little things fascinate me tonight. The way the carpet in the corner of my room curls up; the frosted-looking white paint on my bedroom ceiling; the yellow teddy bear key chain on my red book bag. I think I'll add another key chain—a skull maybe.*

---

I read the paragraph about five times before copying it here, in my digital diary. Her description is frustratingly familiar; I know I have seen a red book bag with a yellow teddy bear key chain. But on whose shoulder?

# 9

## The Source

**In the parking lot of Rynec, Inc.**

Robert Mulligan Middleton's life ambition was to be the greatest hacker in the world. No, not just the world—the entire history of the world, past, present, and future.

He was already well on his way to greatness. Living in Mourning had offered him countless opportunities to practice his skills without getting into too much trouble. But lately his sphere of influence was getting a little cramped. He was ready to expand.

His most recent project was cracking the network at Rynec, Inc. As one of Mourning's largest corporations, it represented a significant challenge—he hoped.

Rob rolled his bike behind some bushes, adjusted his suit jacket, and walked across the Rynec parking lot. He had a clipboard under his arm, a twenty-five-CD case in his hand, and two thumb drives in his pocket. The clipboard was for show, as were most of the CDs in the case. The thumb drives and one or two of the discs were his real weapons—his tools, as he liked to call them.

He walked through the glass double doors and stopped at the front desk. The secretary looked up at him over her glasses. He smiled at her.

"Just dropping something off for—" he consulted his clipboard; "Mrs. Thelma Andrews?"

"She's right back there." The secretary pointed at another glass door.

Apparently she didn't think him worth escorting, and Rob was fine with that. Mrs. Andrews was out for an hour, taking her son to the dentist. All he wanted to do was leave a CD and a note on her desk.

Rob found Mrs. Andrews' desk easily and placed the CD and note on her keyboard tray, hidden from her coworkers but impossible for her to miss once she returned. Then he left, nodding pleasantly to the secretary on his way out.

In the note he had written a short set of instructions, supposedly from Rynec's IT department. If Mrs. Andrews followed the instructions, she would insert the CD and install both the harmless software update and the Trojan he had piggybacked onto it. And once the Trojan began to work, it would open a port in the Rynec firewall for him.

Rob did not think of himself as a bad guy. He never intended to use the information he gathered to hurt anyone. He was just interested in knowing things. Someday perhaps the things that he knew would make money for him—but for now, he simply wanted to find out what he could do, how far he could stretch himself.

He biked home and played an online game until six o'clock. Then he opened "The Hub," the program he had designed to keep track of all his hacking endeavors. He skimmed through the list of infected computers until he saw Mrs. Andrews's workstation.

She had taken the bait.

"You gotta love human beings." he said aloud. "So gullible."

"Who's gullible?" said a voice behind him.

He minimized the window and spun around in his chair. "Micah! What are you doing here?"

Micah shrugged. "Hangin' out."

"Okay, well, give me a minute."

"Okay." But Micah did not move from the doorway.

Rob rolled his eyes. "My mom's got some ice cream sandwiches in the freezer. How about you bring us a couple."

"Okay." Micah turned and disappeared.

Rob sighed, shaking his head. Micah was a genius with computers—not so good at reading people. And Rob knew that an understanding of both was necessary to greatness.

He closed down his program. He allowed his band of Info Addicts to see the results of some of his hacking endeavors, but a project like this was too big. Not all of the guys in his group were as careful as he, or had as much respect for guarding information. Rob stole secrets, but he kept them too.

By the time Micah returned with the ice cream sandwiches, Rob had a music website up on his screen instead of "The Hub."

"So what's up, dude?" he asked.

Micah shrugged. "I was thinking of emailing Nikki."

Rob pushed his chair back from the desk. "Why?"

"She's cute."

Rob laughed. "Well, you've got to have more to say than that."

"Why do you think I came to see you?"

"You don't need me, man," said Rob. "Just be yourself. What do you want to say to her?"

Micah unwrapped his sandwich. "I could tell her about the drawings in the bathroom."

"Okay, maybe you do need me," said Rob. "Look, man, don't start out with that. Be cool, not gross. Here, I'll open a new email, and we can work on it together."

After half an hour, they sent a very short, very friendly email to Nikki's school account. It had Micah's name at the end, but Rob had written most of the words.

"Do you think she'll reply?"

"Sure she will. She's cool."

Rob did not tell Micah that he had saved some of the best lines for his own email to Nikki. After Micah left, he wrote to her.

*Hey Nikki,*

*Just wondering how your info-gathering is going. Let me know if u need anything—I am your Source for all things.*

*Rob*

Half an hour later, he checked his email again and found that she had responded.

*Hey Rob,*

*Thanks for the offer to help. Who do you think could have sent those emails at school? Everybody else seems to think it's a prank. I'm not sure.*

*Nikki*

Rob leaned back in his chair. Whether he thought there was any danger to the school or not, he wanted to keep this conversation going as long as possible. What could he say that would pique Nikki's interest?

After a few minutes, he began typing. *I don't think it's just a prank. I think somebody is mad at the school. Maybe someone getting bad grades, or their girlfriend broke up with them, or something.*

He sent the email and waited. In a few minutes, Nikki's response popped up on his screen. *I guess people get pretty mad over breakups. You'd think they would be mad at the person, not the school, though. How about you? Has anyone ever broken up with you?*

He grinned and typed.

*No, I broke up with her.*

It was true, he had broken up with Lana first, but only because he hacked into her instant-messaging account and found out that she was planning to break up with him the next day. He had beaten her to it, a fact he was immensely proud of.

Nikki replied to his email almost instantly.

*Good for you. Did you do it by email or text?*

*Of course not,* Rob typed. *I did it in person. What kind of lame dude breaks up with a girl by email or text?*

Nikki replied, *LOL! Good 4 u. So let me know if u get any more bad vibes. kk?*

Rob could tell that she was signaling the end of the conversation. *I will. CU @ school. Over & out.*

It was the longest email conversation he'd had with a girl in quite a while. That, plus the wealth of information that had just opened for him at Rynec, made Rob feel very pleased with himself.

He would sleep well tonight.

# 10

## Broken Circle

---

### Nikki's Digital Diary
<Posted Saturday, October 8, 9:40 p.m.>

---

Yesterday was the most horrible day of my life to date.

I don't really feel like writing about it, but if I don't, I think I might explode. So I'll try . . .

---

My sixth sense tells me when something big is about to change. And as I walked up to the door of my house yesterday afternoon, I felt change. The air was charged with it.

*Something is going on here*, I thought.

I opened the door and saw my dad sitting on the floor of the hall, crying.

"Dad!" I ran to him. "What is it? Is someone—"

He handed me a letter, two sheets of paper folded into thirds. It was typed, but the first sentence gave away the author as surely as handwriting would have.

*Dave,*

*By the time you read this, I'll be gone.*

## The Silent

I read the letter from beginning to end. It was no longer than it needed to be. Mom had left Dad—left us. She said that she wanted to be free . . . to be happy.

Some parts of the letter were so intensely personal that I skimmed over them. I knew that in his right mind Dad would never have let me read those paragraphs, so I read only what I had to, to help my brain understand. My heart would never understand.

I read the last line of Mom's note again. *I thought it would be easier for all of us this way. No goodbyes, no tears.*

No tears? Who was she kidding? There were tears streaming down my face and Dad's. She just hadn't wanted to see them.

Dad and I held onto each other and cried. I have never seen him cry like that, and it frightened me so much that I held back my own sobs, hoping that would calm him. I wanted to ask him why he was crying so hard. Of course it was a shock, but he and Mom were heading for trouble. They haven't been getting along for years, and over the past several months it has been much worse. Dad tried to fix it. He took her to the beach for a week in August; but when they came home, nothing had changed. They still argued constantly. Sometimes Mom even slept on the couch, though she tried to hide the fact from us kids by getting up early.

But I can remember a time, years ago, when Dad touched Mom's cheek and kissed her when he came home from work. I remember how they used to massage each other's feet while they watched TV after dinner. Sometimes they would argue over whose feet were the smelliest. And they would laugh.

That was long ago. As I watched Dad cry, I thought maybe he was remembering those times, wondering where he had gone wrong—what he could have done to change the present.

When he calmed down, I asked, "Does Tae know?"

Dad nodded. "He came back before I did."

"Where is he?"

"In his room." He sighed and went into the kitchen. I heard the water running and knew he was washing the tears from his face. He was ashamed of them.

A sudden thought struck me, and I ran upstairs to Mom and Dad's room. I yanked open her drawers, one after the other, and threw open the closet. Her things were gone. All of them.

She had moved some of the stuff alone, little by little. Other things she had put into big plastic garbage bags, so that I would not know what I was carrying when I helped her take them out to the car.

Pain and anger seared through me. She wanted to avoid a scene, so she lied to me. She used me to help her get away.

I couldn't see through my tears. "I hate you!" I whispered to the empty room. "How could you do this to me?"

In the letter Mom had said that she only stayed this long because of me. She wanted to wait until I was old enough to "handle" it. But if she really cared about my feelings, she wouldn't have tricked me into carrying her things to the car for her.

I had never been so angry and hurt in my life. I took the pillow from Mom's side of the bed and threw it against the wall. Then I picked it up and threw it again, and again, as hard as I could. I threw it so hard that the pillow finally burst at the corner and sprinkled feathers over the carpet. Sinking to the floor, I set my back against the bureau and cried.

I sat there for an hour or more, too hurt to move or think. Finally I picked up the ruined pillow, stuffed most of the feathers back in, and carried it downstairs.

Dad was sitting at the kitchen table doing paperwork. His nose and eyes were still red.

Then the doorbell rang, and Tae thundered down the stairs. "I'll get it!"

I heard someone say "I have two pizzas here for a Taylor Altemann?"

Dad and I looked at each other.

"Pizza?" I said. "He ordered pizza?"

Dad shrugged.

A moment later Tae came into the kitchen carrying two medium pizzas. He set them on the counter. We stared at him.

"I figure we have to eat," Tae said. "Nobody's going to feed us."

He flicked open one of the boxes and pulled out a piece of pizza. The cheese stretched until he broke it off and wound the strings around his finger.

"Anyone feel like saying grace?"

I expected Dad to nod and bow his head, but he did not. The muscles in his jaw tightened, and he went back to his papers, writing a row of numbers in a blank space. I tried to find the will to pray, but my head was churning with too much anger and pain. I couldn't make myself close my eyes and say the words, *Thank you, Lord.*

Tae looked from Dad to me and nodded. "I didn't think so," he said, and bit into his slice.

I waited for the smell of the pizza to sicken me, but it didn't. In fact my stomach growled.

"Got any pepperoni with olives?" I asked.

He slid aside the first box and opened the second. "Right here, sis."

I tore a slice free from the second pizza and bit into it. We ate in silence until Tae's eyes fixed on the destroyed pillow beside the kitchen trash can.

"What's with the pillow?" he said.

"I beat it up."

He raised his eyebrows. "Yeah? Did it help?"

"Yup. You should try it."

"Dad, you want any pizza?" Tae asked.

"No, I'm fine."

"Come on, Dad," I said. "I know you're hungry. Have a piece."

Tae slapped a slice onto a plate and set it down next to Dad.

My dad stared at the pizza for a minute. At last he picked it up and sank his teeth in.

"Better?" I said.

He gave me a half-nod.

After several minutes of chewing, Dad said, "You kids think I should call Rick Berkell?"

The only time Tae had come to church with me and Dad, he had spent the entire hour shifting his weight and stretching his legs and looking immensely bored. Afterwards he shared several biting comments about the Berkells' personal lives and the inconsistencies he thought he saw in them. Dad had gotten so angry that he and Tae nearly came to blows. We never brought Tae with us to worship again.

Bringing up Mr. Berkell at a volatile time like this was not a good idea. I waited, wondering how Tae would react.

But he surprised me. "Dad, if he can help you, go for it," he said. "Me, I can deal with stuff in my own way." He took another slice of pizza and went up to his room.

"What do you think, Nikki?" said Dad.

I settled onto a kitchen chair. "I think you should call him. This is a weird situation, you know?" I heard my voice getting higher and thinner, threatening to break, so I took a moment to steady it. "You need somebody wise that can give you advice."

He nodded. "I think I'll go upstairs and call him now."

He left everything on the table—laptop, papers, and half-eaten pizza. I couldn't bear to stay in the silent kitchen, so I took my school bag to the living room. I set up a folding table in front of the couch, dug my homework out of my bag, and turned on the TV.

*Look, Mom*, I thought. *I'm doing homework in front of the TV like you always told me not to. Come and stop me.*

Of course, she didn't, not even when I brought out two more slices of pizza on a plate so I could eat *and* do homework *and* watch TV, all at the same time.

The TV and homework thing worked for a while. But at last it was eleven o'clock. I knew I would have to face my room sooner or later, and I would rather sleep up there than in the big empty living room. So I took my stuff upstairs, got ready for bed as quickly as I could, hopped in, and shut my eyes.

# The Silent

Sleep is a fickle thing. It always overpowers you when you least want it to, like when you're trying to study for a test. But when you plead for it, when you need it to blot out your thoughts and your memories and your pain—then it refuses to come.

Right before midnight I gave up trying to sleep and called Haley.

"Huh?" she answered. I had woken her up.

"I need to talk to you." As soon as I said the words, I felt the tears coming again, tying up all the muscles in my nose and throat.

"Okay, sure. Just give me a second to wake up."

I loved Haley. "It's about my mom. She left today."

"Left? As in—"

"As in never coming back."

"Oh," said Haley. "Oh, Nikki, that's harsh. Are you okay? I mean, obviously you're not okay, but . . . how are you doing?"

"Um," I said, and then I burst into tears. Haley made all sorts of sympathetic noises to take the place of the hugs and hand-squeezes I would have gotten if she'd been in the room with me. When it was over, I felt, not necessarily better, but at least relieved. And tired. Very, very tired.

"You better get some rest," said Haley. "We'll talk about it tomorrow."

"Okay."

"And when you're feeling up to it, I know something that will make it better."

I knew she wanted me to say "what?" so I made an effort and said it.

"Shopping!" she said. "Doesn't that sound like fun?"

# 11

## Black Water

Haley means well. She thinks that a shopping spree can cure all ills, or at least drive them into the background for a while. I, on the other hand, would rather watch a movie or read a book in the privacy of my bedroom. But that, according to Haley, is a slippery slope that leads to moping and depression. She's probably right. I keep a box of tissues beside my bed all the time now for the silent hours of the night.

It embarrasses me that I cried so much for Mom this past week. After all, I'm not five years old. I'm seventeen going on eighteen, practically an adult. And it's not as though Mom has died. She is still breathing and walking and working. I could get a ride to her workplace and see her anytime I want to. But would she want to see me?

I knew or feared that something like this would happen. But the way it happened was so wrong in every way. I couldn't get over it. I just kept crying.

# The Silent

Yesterday, a week after Mom left, I asked Haley if she wanted to go to the mall after school. She was enthusiastic, of course.

"Is it all right if I invite a couple of other people?" she asked.

It wasn't, but I said, "Okay."

I rode the bus home. A few minutes after I finished changing my clothes, Haley pulled up in her mom's car and honked. I hurried down and squeezed into the back seat next to Sharonda and Arisha. A girl I didn't know sat in the front seat next to Haley.

"Nikki, this is Mel," said Haley. "Her family just moved in a couple doors down from mine. She goes to St. Mary's Catholic School."

Mel looked at me in the rearview mirror and waved. I faked a smile. "Nice to meet you."

"Okay then. We're off!" sang Haley.

We drove the forty-five minutes to the mall, ate at the food court, and spent the next few hours wandering in and out of stores. Sharonda and Mel turned out to be "clothes freaks" who had to try on every cute top or flattering pair of pants in every shop. Haley didn't care. She can be happy anywhere with anybody, but Arisha and I were bored out of our skins. We stood at the entrance to MyShape Shop, waiting while Mel agonized over her budget and yet another pair of capris.

"There's a music and video store over there." Arisha pointed. "Want to go?"

"Sure."

We left without telling the others where we were going—a stupid mistake. Half an hour later I tried calling Haley to find out where we should meet them. Her voicemail picked up at once.

I turned to Arisha. "Haley's phone is turned off. Do you have the number for either one of those other girls?"

She shook her head. "I just met them tonight."

I groaned. "Great."

"Maybe she'll call you," said Arisha.

"Unless her cell battery died."

Arisha winced. "So do we stay here or look for them?"

72

I know if you're lost in the forest, the rule is to stay put till someone finds you. That rule never made much sense to me, and anyway I figured it didn't apply to malls.

"Let's look for them," I said. "They can't have gone far. The mall isn't that big."

We looked until our feet were sore and the mall was about to close. Normally I would have been mildly frustrated or laughed it off, but my emotions were already so fragile that I was nearly in tears.

"We can meet them at the car," suggested Arisha. "They'll have to head there when the mall closes."

We went outside and waited in the dark parking lot until nine-thirty when the mall doors locked. Still no Haley. I was getting nervous. Strange people hung out in the mall parking lot at night, and I could see three of them from where we stood by the car. They were watching Arisha and me.

"Do have any pepper spray?" I whispered.

"No. You?"

I shook my head and took out my cell phone. "I'm calling my brother."

But Tae did not answer his phone. If I called Dad, he would freak out. And I didn't want that, so I dialed Justin's number.

He picked up on the third ring. "Hey, what's up?"

"Hey Justin, I'm in the mall parking lot with Arisha, and it's dark, and there are three scary men here."

"What? I thought you were with Haley and some other girls."

"We got separated, and Haley's phone is off."

"Well, the mall's closed by now, right? They have to come back to the car."

"I know that," I said. "But they're not coming."

"I don't know what you want me to do, Nikki. I'm almost an hour away."

"Yeah, well, I just wanted to call somebody, and Tae didn't answer his phone," I said.

"You'll be fine," said Justin. "They have mall security. Just sit tight till Haley and the others show up, okay? I have to go. See you Monday."

He hung up. I was even closer to tears now. In fact I think I would have started bawling right there if Arisha hadn't tapped my arm.

"I think I see them," she said.

A security guard was letting Haley, Mel, and Sharonda out one of the department store doors. They were all laughing as if being locked inside the mall was a truly hilarious thing.

"Where were you?" I said to Haley when they reached us. "I tried calling."

"Sorry, my battery died," she said, opening the trunk so everyone could put their purchases inside. "Did you and Arisha have fun?"

"Lots." I climbed into the back seat and stared silently out the window for the ride back to Mourning, clutching the CD I had bought.

On our way back into Mourning, we passed through the shady section of town, the part that housed places like the bar "Blue Light, Black Water" and a place whose sign simply read "The Drink." As we drove past the Drink, I saw a young man staggering through the parking lot. Something about his drunken movements seemed familiar.

"Wait a minute," I said. "That looks like—"

It was too dark to be sure, but it looked like my brother.

"Turn around!" I yelled. "Go back!"

"What?" Haley slammed on her brakes, and the car behind her honked.

"That's Tae! Back there in that parking lot."

"Calm down, Nikki!" She did a U-turn and pulled into the Drink's parking lot. "If my parents saw me anywhere near this place—"

I hopped out of the car and took a second look at the man. "It is Tae, and there's his car. It looks like he's going to need someone to drive him home. You guys go on."

"Are you sure?"

"Positive. I'll be fine."

I shut the door before she could protest and ran to my brother. He was leaning against the side of his car, peering at his key ring.

"Tae?"

He tried to focus on my face. "Hey, sis."

"You're drunk," I said.

The horror in my voice did not phase him. "So what?" He staggered forward and poked his key at the car door.

"Tae-man, you shouldn't be driving," said a voice behind me.

I whirled. The young man who had just arrived looked about five years older than me. Though he was not as drunk as my brother, I could smell the alcohol on his breath.

"Are you a friend of his?" I asked.

"Yeah."

"Well, I'm his sister. And I'm taking him home."

"You have a license, kid?"

"Yes," I snapped. "Help me get him in the car."

I took one of Tae's arms, and his friend took the other. "Come on, Tae," I said. "We're going home."

"Good," he said. "I feel kinda . . . sick."

"You got a bag or something in there?" asked the friend. "He might need it."

"Don't worry about us," I said. "You've done enough."

"You sure?"

"Just go!"

"Okay!" He backed away, holding up his hands.

I buckled Tae's seat belt, shut the car door, and went around to the other side. The "friend" was shuffling back towards the bar.

"Hey!" I yelled.

He turned.

# The Silent

"Don't ever speak to my brother again. Don't call him; don't email him. Don't invite him out for so much as a soda. If you do, I'll find a way to hurt you. I promise."

"Yeah, whatever," he said, backing towards the bar again.

"And you can pass that along to all his other drinking buddies too!"

I got in the car and slammed the door. My stomach hurt, and my hands were shaking so badly I couldn't start the car. I leaned my forehead against the steering wheel and took several deep breaths.

"We goin' somewhere or what?" said Tae.

I looked at him. His skin was white, and sweat glazed his forehead. "You look awful," I said.

"Well, I'm wasted," he said, with a ghastly grin.

"Idiot," I said.

"I'm not an idiot."

"Yes, you are." I started the car and headed out of the parking lot.

When we reached home, I led Tae upstairs to his room.

"I want to lie down." He pushed past me and closed the door in my face.

"Okay," I said to the door. Then I went to my room, curled up on my bed, and cried.

Lots of the kids at Mourning High would have thought nothing of the incident. They might even have laughed. But Tae is my big brother. When we were younger he was a pain in the neck, but he protected me too. He allowed no one to bully me.

Tonight he was someone else—someone vulnerable, even repulsive. Someone who needed my help.

My tears have turned into fury now, though I'm not sure who deserves my anger. Maybe Dad, because he does nothing to help Tae anymore. Maybe Mom, because she left us all. Maybe Tae's loser friends.

Or maybe God.

Why didn't He save Tae when He saved me?

## Nikki's Digital Diary
<Posted Sunday, October 16, 4:12 p.m.>

This morning Dad and I went to church. Dad didn't want to go, but Mr. Berkell told him it was essential to keep his family in church in spite of the breakup.

Mrs. Land wasn't there. Haley's mom said she was ill with the flu. I was so disappointed my throat tightened up, but I got control of myself and decided to talk to Mrs. Berkell instead. Maybe she would give me help instead of platitudes this time.

---

After the service I went up to her. "Could I talk to you for a minute, Mrs. Berkell?"

"Of course, Nikki. Come with me."

She led me into the dining room. In its center stood a ponderous dining table, surrounded by six chairs with white seat cushions. An antique grandfather clock ticked softly in the silence. I eyed the corner cabinet where the china was displayed in neat rows. My grandmother had a china cabinet just like that.

"Have a seat, Nikki."

The heavy wooden chairs were hard to move on the thick carpet, but I managed to pull one out far enough to sit in it. Mrs. Berkell sat down across from me and waited.

"I guess I'm just wondering . . ." I felt the tears coming and raged at myself for being so emotional. "I'm not sure what to do about Mom leaving. It's a lot to handle."

"You need to cast your burden upon the Lord," said Mrs. Berkell. "He will sustain you."

I clenched my hands together, trying to hold the tears back. "What does that mean exactly?"

"What does what mean?"

"That verse. You're quoting the Bible, right? What does it mean, 'cast your burden on the Lord?' How does a person do that?"

# The Silent

Mrs. Berkell shifted her weight in the chair. "You pray about it, and then just let the Lord take the burden. Ask Him to restore your joy."

*Joy?* I felt a twinge of anger.

"Ever since Mom left, I can't really pray," I said. "When I try to, the only thing I can really do is ask why. Why did He let this happen?"

"Sometimes God does things that we don't understand," she said. "We have to accept that He knows best. Ours is not to reason why."

That phrase never made any sense to me. Of course it is "ours to reason why." That's what makes us different from animals— the ability to wonder about things. God intends for us to ask why. Maybe He doesn't always have to give us an answer, but He does want us to ask. If we never asked "why," we'd never discover anything.

"Nikki?" Mrs. Berkell frowned, and I realized that I had been staring into nothing, occupied with my own thoughts.

"Dad's probably ready to go," I said. "Thanks for the talk."

"Anytime." She smiled.

---

Maybe it was wrong of me to leave her with the impression that her "advice" had helped. But I didn't know how to enlighten her without seeming rude. I know that she means well and that she loves God and other people. And I'm sure that she has a lot of "life experience" to draw from when she is advising others. But somehow she manages to keep herself separate from her advice. Maybe that's what makes her wisdom so cold and comfortless.

# 12

## Taylor

In the kitchen of the Altemann house

Nikki was worried about him.

Taylor could see it in her eyes when she greeted him in the morning. There was a searching look in them, as if she were trying to pry open his soul and find out what hid there. He couldn't help turning away whenever he saw that look.

Nikki went down to the kitchen early every morning now to make toast and pour orange juice and set out the cereal. The first time she did it, he thought it was just a one-time thing. But then she did it again the next day, and the next.

"You can't be Mom, you know," he told her one morning.

Nikki looked at him and said, "I wouldn't want to be."

There was something in her eyes these days, and not just the searching or the sadness. They looked older, deeper—not like a seventeen-year-old's. And the way she had handled the situation that night, when he was so drunk—she had acted as if she were his elder, instead of the other way around.

She was different, he thought. And not just because Mom had left. There was something else on her mind.

# The Silent

They used to be close before he graduated and went off to try college. He never admitted it to his friends, but he missed Nikki more than anything else at home. Sure, she could be annoying, but she wasn't so bad as some guys' sisters. She liked video games as well as novels, and she could talk intelligently about computers. And she didn't giggle as much as some girls did.

What was it with girls and giggling? He had expected college girls to be different from high school girls, but they turned out to be almost as giggly and twice as ridiculous, as if college, to them, were nothing but a gigantic manhunt, instead of the place to train for a future career.

His professors had disgusted him too. Half of them weren't qualified to be teaching their courses no matter what their degrees said; and the other half were brilliant in their subject but had no idea how to communicate knowledge to others. So Tae had quit.

And his parents had fussed at him. They had tried to argue him into going back. Sometimes he almost convinced himself to do it, but he had no idea what he would major in other than something generic like business or humanities.

And then Mom had left.

It was just another snapped link in his broken world. Another ideal crushed. He had known that his parents' marriage was unsteady, but that didn't make the blow any easier to take. It shook him up and made him realize that he needed some direction in life—somewhere to go. And when he had nearly driven himself crazy trying to figure something out, Casey had called and invited him out for drinks.

He remembered going to the bar and drinking, and drinking more. And then everything was a blur of dizziness and nausea and tilting pavement . . . and Nikki's horrified face.

Taylor could see her face in his mind as clearly as he could see the box of cereal in front of him.

His father strode through the kitchen and poured coffee into the mug he always carried to work.

"Nikki's gone?"

Tae nodded. "Already off to school."

"So what's on the menu for you? Another productive day of gaming?"

Tae crumpled his napkin. "Quit pushing me, okay?"

"You need a job, son."

"Yeah, I know."

"No, you don't." His father leaned toward him, and Tae reluctantly looked him in the eyes. "I need you to get a job."

It took Tae a moment to understand. "We need the money?"

"Yes. With your mother gone—"

"Don't sweat it," said Tae, standing up. "I understand."

He was oddly excited. Finally he had a purpose. He wouldn't just be job-hunting to add to the general pool of funds. Dad and Nikki actually needed him.

"I'll work up a resume," he said. "And I'll look around online. See what's available. Is your company hiring?"

"Sorry, no. They just laid off some guys; I don't think we'll be hiring anytime soon." His father moved toward the kitchen door. "I'm just praying they won't lay off anyone else. It's a tough market out there right now."

"Must be, when you have to depend on a minimum-wage type like me to help out," said Tae.

His father smiled—his first real one in days.

"See you tonight, son."

"See you."

Tae went to the bathroom and looked at himself in the mirror. The scruffy dark growth along his jaw would have to go, and he would have to gel his hair. Add to that a dress shirt and a little cologne, and anyone would be glad to hire him.

He grinned at himself in the mirror. "Operation Transformation has begun," he said aloud.

Secretly he had always liked one of Nikki's chick flicks where a girl finds out she's a princess and undergoes a metamorphosis from gawky teen to beauty queen. He hummed one of the songs from the movie in his head as he shaved and trimmed and gelled.

# The Silent

After half an hour, he had achieved the level of class he wanted.

"Tae-man, you are lookin' good," he said to his reflection. "Now for a shirt and pants to go with the new look."

He went to his room and picked his way through the piles of clothes and trash that littered the carpet. He knew he was old enough to clean up after himself, but since Mom left, he had let everything go. Maybe he was trying to punish her somehow. He could see the similarity between his own lack of discipline and Nikki's desperate efforts to keep everything running the way it did under Mom's regime.

As he passed his computer, he glanced at the bookshelf beside it. The shelves were lined with games—a collection worthy of a master gamer. For a moment he was tempted to sit down and lose himself in one of the elaborate story lines he loved. If only life could be like a game: a map to guide you on your quest, all the excitement you wanted, and the certainty of resurrection if you made a deadly mistake.

He pulled on a maroon and white striped shirt and a pair of grey jeans. Then he sat down at the computer to freshen up his old high school resume. It was discouraging that he couldn't put any degree under the "Education" section of the resume. He hadn't even completed a year of college.

At last he headed out the door and climbed into his car, a stack of resumes in a folder under his arm. This was how he liked to do things, not planned ahead for months, but suddenly, on a whim. It kept life exciting.

But life liked to turn his expectations upside down.

It was Monday, and the managers at most of the businesses he entered were either absent or too busy to speak with him. He had to settle for leaving a resume in the hands of one of the employees with a wild hope that the person would actually lay it on the boss's desk instead of tossing it in the trash.

He was glad to learn that there was a manager on duty at Soza's. Mr. Clyne had known Tae for years.

"So, what are you up to?" said Mr. Clyne, glancing at the folder under Tae's arm. "Fundraising?"

"Job hunting actually," said Tae.

Mr. Clyne's smile stiffened. "Job hunting? At Soza's?"

Tae forced a grin. "Yes, that's right."

"Well, I wish I could help you there, Taylor, but as you know, we hire mostly high school students—part-time workers."

"Sure," said Tae. "I understand."

"Now, you're a college man," continued Mr. Clyne. "You've got a degree, right? So you can look higher than a burger bar like this."

"Right." Tae laughed, but inside he felt hollow.

He went to Rynec, Inc., one of Mourning's largest corporations, but the woman at Human Resources told him that the company had just been through a series of layoffs.

"We're really not hiring right now," she said. Then she tapped his resume with a manicured nail. "And I'm afraid that without a degree your chances would be slim anyway."

"Thanks for your time," said Tae.

He returned to his car and sat in it, staring at the dashboard. He had given out a couple dozen resumes. That just about exhausted the employment opportunities in Mourning.

Maybe he was overlooking some businesses. Or maybe he could look farther away in one of the neighboring towns. If he tried for a job at a restaurant where the manager hadn't known him all his life, he might have better luck.

Right now, he was hungry. He would go home, pick up some food along the way, and bury himself in a game for the evening. He could forget today's humiliation and be someone worth noticing, for a few hours anyway.

He started the car and drove home.

# 13

## Torn Hearts

**Nikki's Digital Diary**
<Posted Tuesday, October 18, 11:12 p.m.>

This evening I convinced Dad to come to the grocery store with me for a big shopping trip. Since Mom left, we have been surviving on take-out with occasional five-minute trips to the nearest drugstore for milk or bread.

At our house, the grocery shopping was always Mom's department. She complained about that frequently, calling it sexist; but whenever Dad or Tae or I went in her place, we ended up buying the wrong brand of pasta or the cream cheese with chives instead of the plain kind.

This shopping trip would be different. There would be no Mom waiting at home to scrutinize everything we bought and tell us what we should have done differently. I found a bitter joy in that. If I wanted to, I could put all my favorite foods into the cart and no one would care.

But that would be childish. I'm the woman of the house now, and I intend to run the place as well as Mom.

I went through the cupboards, the pantry, and the fridge, making a list of everything we would need for the next few weeks. It was a very long, very impressive list.

I showed it to Dad as we walked into the grocery store.

"Any idea how much all of this will cost?" he asked.

I stared at the neat column. "Um . . ."

He sighed. "I'll take that as a 'no.'"

"Sorry."

"Well, we'll just see what happens, I guess."

"I'll keep the receipt so we can look back at it later and see what we paid for everything," I told him.

"Sounds great, honey."

But he began to doubt my list before we had covered half the aisles in the store.

"There are only three of us, hon," he said. "Do we really need five boxes of cereal?"

"But these two are my favorites, and this one's Tae's, and those are yours," I said. "They'll last us all month."

"Then why do we need Pop-Tarts if we're going to be eating cereal every morning?"

"Good point," I said, plunking the Pop-Tarts box back on the shelf.

"And these oranges." He touched the bag of oranges in the cart. "We never eat oranges."

"They're on sale."

"Just because they're on sale doesn't mean we need them, Nik."

I put my hands on my hips. "You want to make the list next time?"

He sighed and rubbed his forehead. I noticed that the grey streaks at his hairline and temples were wider and longer. And his eyes looked so tired.

"I guess we'll just stick to the list," he said.

"Tell you what." I linked my arm with his. "I'll tell you what's on the list, and you tell me what doesn't make sense, and hopefully we'll come out with a decent supply of food."

"Deal."

As we rounded the corner and approached the meat section, I saw a familiar figure bending over the beef. My mother.

My first instinct was to run to her; my second, to hide in the junk food aisle till she was gone.

"Dad," I said.

"I know," he answered. "I see her."

"What should we do?"

His jaw tightened. "I want to talk to her."

He quickened his pace, our half-filled cart rattling in loud protest as we hurtled towards my mother. We had almost reached her when a woman walked out of the frozen section and placed two bags of vegetables in my mother's shopping cart. Probably a friend or coworker—someone Mom was staying with until she got her own place—away from us.

Dad and the shopping cart slowed, but we were too close to back away now. Mom set the package of ground beef in her cart and glanced up. Her face paled, and she muttered something to the woman beside her.

For a moment I hoped they would leave, but they stood their ground, waiting for us. When our cart was alongside theirs, Dad stopped.

"Hello, Dave," said my mother.

"Hello, Julie."

Mom looked at me. "Hey, Nikki. How are you, baby?"

As I met her eyes, I infused into my stare all the pain and anger that I felt. I knew it was wrong. But I wasn't ready to forgive her—not yet.

"Not taking it well, obviously," said the friend. I gave her my most murderous glare.

"This is Muirella," said Mom. "Her husband works with me."

Dad jerked his head once in acknowledgement. For a minute or two we all stood there, frozen.

At last Mom broke the awkwardness with a sigh and a shake of her shoulders. "Go ahead, Dave," she said. "Give me chapter and verse. I know you want to."

"Okay," he said. "Matthew 19:6. 'What God has joined together, let not man separate.'"

My mother shook her head. "Your God is so small."

"No," said Dad. "My God is huge. I can't put words in His mouth. I can't shape Him the way I want him to be."

Muirella laughed. "I can't believe this. You're adults, and you're having a 'my god is bigger than your god' discussion."

Neither of my parents answered her. They stared at each other as if they were the only two people in the world.

"I know I'm to blame for this," said my father. I couldn't believe I was hearing the words. How could he take the blame for her desertion?

"I didn't treat you the way I should have," he continued. "I failed you as a husband."

"Maybe," said Mom. "But that's not the only reason I left."

Dad's voice was soft. "You're still searching, Julie, just like always."

Shaking her head, Mom pushed the shopping cart past us. Muirella followed.

I suppose Muirella was right in a way. Their discussion about the size of God was a bit ridiculous. Dad was trying to take the high ground, but as much as it hurts me to admit it, I know that he is not a strong Christian. He does not always know how to react, or what to say. I can criticize his words all day if I want to; but had I been in his shoes, I doubt that I would have done any better.

I squeezed his arm gently. "We need some meat, Dad."

Sighing, he glanced at the meat bin. "Pick something out, okay? Just not steaks. They're too expensive."

# The Silent

We saw Mom and Muirella again while we were checking out, but they were several stations away, so we did not have to speak to them.

Dad didn't say anything while we loaded the groceries into the trunk, or when we got into the car and pulled out of the parking lot. If I didn't speak up, we would spend the entire drive home in awkward silence; so I said, "That was harder than I thought it would be."

"Really? For me it was easier."

I stared out the window, watching the other cars whoosh past us as we waited to turn left. "Do you think she'll stay in Mourning?"

"Probably. She has a good job here."

"So we'll see her around."

"It's likely."

"Is she going to divorce you?"

"If she does, I'm not fighting it." He shook his head. "There's no point. Our marriage is sunk, Nikki. Has been for months. Done. Over."

"So you're not going to try—"

"What is there to try? She made her choice." He glanced at me. "Do you really want her back after this?"

I shrugged. "She's my mom. Sure, I'm mad at her, but I still love her."

"I don't."

The pain that stabbed through me when he said that was as sharp as it was unexpected. His words seemed so final—no appeals, no retractions. For him, it was over.

"I'm sorry about this, Nikki," he said. "It's never easy."

"You're just going to let her go." My voice, thick with tears and anger, barely sounded like mine.

"Nikki, I don't have a choice, okay?"

"You always have a choice."

"What am I going to do?" he said. "This is the twenty-first century, Nik. If I don't make her happy, Julie has every right to find someone who can."

I was crying openly by then. He softened his tone. "She hasn't made me very happy either, you know."

"You were happy. I remember."

"That was years ago, before—"

"Before what?"

"Before I became a Christian."

I saw the tension in his face. "So, what? You're blaming that?"

"Personal belief is a huge factor in a relationship. When someone changes—I mean, really changes, inside out—the relationship changes. I am a different man than the one she married."

"A better one?"

He heard the note of accusation in my voice. "I try to be, Nikki. You can think whatever you want, but I do try."

I touched his shoulder. "I'm sorry."

Dad sighed. "So am I."

After a few minutes he said, "How's your brother doing?"

"He's okay, I guess. He shaved and fixed his hair yesterday."

"I saw."

"He said he went out job-hunting."

When Dad didn't react, I said, "You knew about the job thing?"

"I asked him to look for one."

"And he actually listened?"

"With your mom gone, we need the extra income. I think he realized that it wasn't me just telling him to get off his seat. It's a matter of need."

Need? I frowned. "Dad, I can get a job and help out too."

"No, I want you to focus on your studies, at least for this first semester. We'll see how it goes after that."

I was relieved. I would have gone to work if he wanted me to, but my homework load is no featherweight right now. During the rest of the drive, I thought about the assignments I had for the

# The Silent

evening. Social studies, trigonometry, English. A lot of reading and a lot of math problems.

When we got home, I helped Dad put the groceries away. We were almost finished when my cell buzzed. It was Kaye.

"I have to take this call, Dad," I said.

He nodded, so I ran upstairs to my room before answering the phone. "Hello?"

"Hi, Nikki. I haven't heard from you in a while."

"I've been busy." I sat down in my big chair and propped my feet on my desk. "There's nothing new to report."

"Okay. So far we have weird drawings in the boys' bathroom, an abusive boyfriend, and a depressed blogger. Am I right?"

"Right." I tried to sound upbeat, but I knew what she meant. Our investigation is going nowhere.

---

As I sit here writing this entry, I can't help but wonder if maybe Luke Larabee is right. Maybe the emails were sent by a prankster. Maybe they have no real purpose behind them.

# 14

## Grins and Lies

### Nikki's Digital Diary
<Posted Wednesday, October 19, 11:38 p.m.>

This morning I got up early to finish my homework. I checked "The Garden of Lost Souls" to see if FourthFate had posted anything new. She hadn't. After that, I checked the mail for the first time in four days. Amid the bills and random junk mail fliers was a packet from Grandma full of information on various prominent colleges.

It doesn't surprise me that she is still on the anti-Christian-college kick. What does surprise me is the fact that she hasn't called, emailed, or written about the divorce. No sympathy, no advice—nothing. She must know about it. She and Mom are so close that I cannot imagine Mom keeping such a big secret from her. I guess it's just one more thing about my grandmother that I can't understand.

---

Haley didn't sit with me on the bus. She looked at me, her eyes cold as a winter sky, and I knew I had done something to offend her. *Great. Just what I need.*

When we got off the bus, I ran to catch up with her.

"Haley, what's wrong with you?"

# The Silent

It probably wasn't the best question to start with. She whirled, her face reddening.

"What's wrong with me? With *me*? You haven't called me or emailed me since Friday night, and you barely said ten words to me yesterday or the day before that."

"I'm sorry," I said. "I was distracted."

"You leave me sitting by myself, you don't call me, you don't ask to study with me, and you wander around school talking to people you've never even said 'hi' to before. And you ask what's wrong with *me*?"

I opened my mouth to answer, but she held up her hand.

"No, don't start. I'm not done. Look, I don't mind your make-new-friends routine; what I *do* mind is the dropping-the-old-friends part. We used to hang out all the time, but the past couple of weeks you have ignored me and shut me out."

I started to speak again, but she went on.

"If this is about your mom, I'm sorry, and I'll try to be understanding once I calm down. But friends are supposed to be there for you during hard times. How can I be there for you if you barely speak to me?"

"Haley—"

"But this isn't about your mom, is it?" Haley said. "It started before that. Maybe it's something I did. Well, if it is, you should tell me, instead of just giving me the cold shoulder. I tried to ask you about it before, and you just brushed me off, so I'm asking again, and if you think I'm—"

"Just stop!" I said. "I can't even get a word in!"

She stopped talking, but she stared at me with those frozen eyes.

"I haven't been ignoring you," I said. "I mean, we went to the mall and stuff. And we see each other every day."

"It's not the same," said Haley. "We used to do homework together and hang out during free period and do stuff on the weekends. Now I'm lucky if you say a dozen words at lunch. You're always busy at night now, doing whatever on your computer. What do you do all evening anyway?"

"Homework," I said. "And blogging. And research."

"Research." She snorted. "Research for what? The English paper isn't due for weeks."

"It's for something else."

"What? What else?"

"I can't tell you."

"Fine." She turned away.

"Oh, come on, Haley." I followed her up the steps.

"I'm not going to be late just to listen to your lame excuses," she said.

I was furious. "All right. If that's the way you want it. See you later . . . maybe."

She didn't answer.

We didn't speak to each other all day, not even at lunch or in the classes where we sat near each other. In social studies I focused on the people sitting ahead of me: Angie Merritt, Eric Frese, Savannah Mason. Savannah fascinated me because she was so thin. Her elbows stuck out sharply, just skin over bones. I remembered hearing a rumor that she was anorexic.

When the bell rang, I realized that I had been so lost in my thoughts that I missed half the lecture. I had only a foggy idea of what the class had been about. Oh well. I would just have to study twice as hard later.

Books and papers rustled as everyone packed up and headed for their next classes. Savannah stood up, hoisting her book bag over her shoulder. She had a red book bag with the little stuffed yellow bear on a key chain hanging from it.

I froze, my eyes fixed on that tiny yellow bear. Words came into my mind. Words I had read so often that I had memorized them.

*Little things fascinate me tonight. The way the carpet in the corner of my room curls up; the frosted-looking white paint on my bedroom ceiling; the yellow teddy bear key chain on my red book bag. I think I'll add another key chain—a skull maybe.*

Savannah was "TheFourthFate."

# The Silent

I jumped up and hurried after her, trying to think of an excuse to talk to her. I had to find out if she was depressed enough to hurt herself—or someone else.

I caught up with her in the hallway.

"Hey, Savannah, do you have the notes from social studies?"

She looked at me as if I had sprouted a second nose. "Why do you need the notes? You were just there."

"Yeah, but I was a little distracted." Which was true.

"I can't give them to you now," she said. "I have class."

"Maybe I could stop by your house tonight and pick them up. Like around seven or eight?" That would be perfect. Maybe I could even get a peek at her room to see if she kept skulls or weapons in there.

"That's really not going to work," she said. "I have a thing starting at eight. An all-evening thing."

"Sure," I said. "I totally understand. I'll check with Angie."

She nodded and quickened her pace, obviously eager to get rid of me.

I let her go, but I was pondering a second plan. What if I shadowed her this evening? Maybe I could find something that would prove whether or not she was the Silent.

Of course, to follow her, I needed a car. Dad's was out of the question, since he would be working late tonight. I couldn't ask Haley for her mom's car, since that would raise too many questions about why I needed it. Besides, Haley would probably say no just out of spite.

That left only one option.

I made myself half a sandwich when I got home and ate it on the way up to Tae's room. He was hunched in front of his computer, playing a video game.

"Hey, Tae. Are you going anywhere tonight?"

"Nope." His eyes did not leave the screen.

"Great! Can I borrow your car?"

"Nope."

"Tae, please. This is really important."

"Important? No. Nothing you have to do could be important enough for me to lend you my car."

I hated to do it, but he left me no choice.

"If you lend me your car, I won't tell Dad about the other night."

He looked at me. "Other night?"

"You were drunk."

"Big deal."

"It would be to Dad. He'd kick you out."

He paused the game and turned to face me. "Are you blackmailing me, little sister?"

"No," I said. "I just really, really need to borrow your car."

He stared at me for a minute or two. Then he slid his hand into his pocket and pulled out his keys. "Just tonight."

"Yes."

"Not a dent, not a ding, not the tiniest scratch."

I rolled my eyes. "Your car has so many dents and scratches you wouldn't even know if I put a new one on it."

"Wanna bet?"

I sighed. "No scratches."

"Fine." He tossed me the keys.

"Yes! Thanks, Tae!"

I raced down the stairs and out to the driveway. If I hurried, I could make it to Savannah's house before she left.

I reached the Mason house several minutes before eight, parked a few driveways down the street, and waited.

At eight twelve by the car's digital clock, Savannah came out of the house and sat down on the swing, purse in hand.

She was waiting for someone to pick her up. But who?

Suddenly I wondered if I had gone too far in my investigation. What if Savannah were the Silent? What if she had an adult accomplice, someone with guns?

A car glided past mine and halted at the curb. Savannah jumped up and climbed into the passenger side. Quickly I took out my phone and wrote the license plate number in a text message. The number looked familiar.

I looked up again, squinting at the plate. That was Justin's car. And it was disappearing around a bend.

I started my car and followed.

I knew enough from spy novels and movies to stay far behind them. Traffic in Mourning at 8 p.m. is fairly light, so it was easy to keep the car in view.

When they turned onto Merrillee Road, I began to understand. Merrillee Road is long and winding, bordered by thick woods. Innumerable small roads branch off from it, some of them abandoned. It's a favorite area for young couples to park at night.

For a moment I refused to believe what my brain was telling me. Justin was my crush, my role model. He was the perfect Christian guy. He would never bring a girl out here.

The fact that Savannah's secret meeting was nothing more than a steamy date was depressing, but it did not bother me half as much as Justin's betrayal. I was so busy trying to process what was happening that I did not notice Justin's car slowing down until I was nearly on its tail. The lights flashed once, twice.

Great. He had seen me. Now what?

He pulled over, and I parked behind him. He stormed towards my car, his face a mask of shock and anger.

I climbed out, my stomach knotting. I had never seen him so furious.

"Nikki! What are *you* doing here?" he said.

"How about you?" I asked.

I hoped he would explain, that he would say he had been taking Savannah shopping, or to a relative's house. I could buy either one of those excuses.

But he said, "Why are you spying on me?"

I clenched my teeth, trying to hold back tears. "I can't tell you."

"Then I'll tell you." His face was inches from mine. A few hours ago the nearness would have thrilled me, but now it was frightening.

"It's because you're obsessed," he said. "You're stalking me."

"No," I said.

"Don't deny it. You think I haven't noticed that you've been crushing on me since fourth grade? You're tailing me because you're jealous."

So he had noticed. Hooray for me.

"It's not because of that," I said. "I was following you because I thought—"

But I couldn't tell him what I had suspected. I couldn't tell him that I was really following Savannah.

"I thought you were up to something," I finished.

"I knew it!" He struck the hood of my car with his fist. "Jealous."

For a moment my care for him overcame my hurt. "Justin, she's not a Christian," I said. "And even if she was, what you're doing is wrong. You know that."

"Are you going to tell on me?"

I couldn't look at him, so I looked away, into the dark woods. "I don't know."

He sighed, and the anger in his face receded a little.

"Come on, Nikki. We've been friends for years," he said. "I won't do it again, okay? Just don't tell my parents."

I chewed on my lower lip. "Okay," I said. "I won't tell on you. That's not my job. But I am going to pray for you. And I'm going to tell Haley, so she can pray too."

"That's great. You two enjoy your prayer party."

He walked back to his car, slammed the door, and roared away, heading back toward town. As the car sped past me, I saw Savannah's pale face in the window.

---

I can still see her face in my mind. I hope Justin knows who he's dealing with. If Savannah is TheFourthFate—and I'm 99 percent sure that she is—then she's really emotionally fragile. Definitely the wrong type of girl for a boy to take out to Merrillee Road. Not that there is a *right* type of girl for that kind of tryst.

# The Silent

I'm still angry that Justin thinks I was tailing him out of jealousy. At least I can be pretty sure that he won't tell anyone about it. I don't want the reputation of a stalker.

I meant to call Haley before going to bed, but then I remembered that she's still mad at me. And I'm not ready to apologize for something that isn't my fault just to get her to talk to me again. She'll get tired of sulking eventually and apologize to me for being so catty and hypersensitive.

# 15

## *Justin*

## In Justin Miller's car

Justin seethed as he drove Savannah home. Nikki had followed him. She had tailed his car, and then she had the audacity to tell him that *he* was in the wrong. She had no right to tell him what he should or should not do.

After a while he realized that Savannah wasn't talking. That in itself wasn't unusual; she had barely said a word when he took her out to dinner the night before. But after the encounter with Nikki, he had expected her to say something.

But she sat white-faced and silent, her right hand gripping the shoulder strap of her seat belt.

Her silence began to annoy him. He would have preferred some kind of outburst, anger or tears or at least frustration. At last, when he couldn't stand it any more, he broke the quiet.

"I'm taking you home," he said. Of course it was obvious.

Still she said nothing.

"I'm sorry about Nikki," he said. "She's kind of emotional and clingy. She believes we're destined for each other or something."

"What do you believe?"

# The Silent

He glanced at her. She was staring straight ahead still clutching the seat belt. Though she did not look at him, he knew she was talking about more than Nikki and her crush.

"I don't know what I believe," said Justin. "I was raised with a certain set of rules—certain standards, you know. But lately I've been testing other waters. There's a lot of world out there."

"Yes," said Savannah. "It's frightening."

"Not really," he said. "So many new things to try, so many ways of living. So many religions. Sometimes I wonder if anyone knows the best way. I mean, does anyone really know what truth is?"

"No," said Savannah after a pause. "I guess not."

Justin turned down her street. This evening had turned out to be so different from what he had intended—not that he really knew what he intended. He had asked Savannah out for the first time the night before, choosing her because she was quiet and pretty and wouldn't gossip about him to other girls. He knew she had few friends.

Their date had gone well. Justin found her strange, but attractive. He had been breaking his parents' rules in little ways for months, and he was ready to take a bigger step away from their moral code and into his own. So he asked her out again, mentioning Merrillee Road; and she had accepted, knowing what that road meant to teen couples.

Her "yes" had surprised him a little, since she hadn't been very animated on their first date. He told himself that his overpowering charm was the reason she accepted, though a voice in his heart whispered otherwise. He had been waiting for this second date all day, and now he was driving Savannah home, not even an hour after picking her up.

"I'm sorry this happened," he said again.

Savannah shook herself a little and loosened her grip on the seatbelt. "It's all right," she said. "It wasn't meant to be."

He pulled up to the curb outside her house. "What are you going to tell your mom?"

"She won't ask." Savannah opened the car door and slid out. "Thanks."

As she went up the walk, Justin's frustration surged again and he hit the steering wheel with his fist. The horn honked, and Savannah turned back, startled. To cover his outburst, Justin waved and kissed his hand to her.

He half-expected his parents to be waiting for him in the living room when he reached home. He thought maybe Nikki had called them by now and told them what a horrible sinner their son was. A vision of the argument that would follow made him want to drive far, far away from Mourning and never come back.

But he didn't have enough money to run away—and he didn't want to leave all his things behind. So he parked the car, pocketed the keys, and stalked up to the front door. His father's car was not in the driveway; he was probably working late again.

"Hey, Justin," called his mom from the kitchen as he passed. "How was study group?"

"We finished early." He hurried upstairs before she could pry. She meant well, but like most mothers she was cursed with an annoying hunger for details about his life.

Justin locked his bedroom door and sprawled in his big desk chair, tapping the power button of his computer with his foot. The machine purred to life, and he relaxed, tilting his head back and closing his eyes. After a minute or two, he put in his password, adjusted his headphones, and typed in the URL of the website he wanted. He did not dare bookmark it, in case his dad somehow discovered his computer password and started poking around.

"Justin?"

How his mother's voice could carry up the stairs, past the locked door, and through his massive headphones was a mystery to Justin. He did not move. Maybe she wouldn't call again.

"Justin!"

He threw the headphones off, shoved back his chair, and yanked the door open. "What?"

"Come down here, please."

# The Silent

Sighing, he went downstairs. His mother stood in the hall, facing his father, who had just come in the front door.

"What is it?" said Justin. "What's so import—"

His eyes fell to the object in his father's hands, and he stopped. It was a box. A box full of papers, picture frames, a pen holder, a coffee mug, and a desk lamp. A box full of everything from his father's desk at work.

"Dad?"

"I, uh," His father cleared his throat. "The . . . the company's been doing some restructuring. Layoffs. Tossing the dead weight overboard." His face crumpled suddenly, and Justin's mother stepped forward.

"Justin, the box," she said.

Justin took the box and set it on the floor. His mom led his father into the living room, to the big red couch, and they cried together for a while.

"I'm sorry," said his dad at last, wiping his eyes. "I want to be strong and trust God. It's just a big shock."

"Dad, you don't have to be a superhero Christian all the time," Justin said. "I know you're not, and that's okay. Nobody's perfect; not you and not me."

"I never claimed to be perfect," said his father. "And I don't expect you to be either."

Justin glanced at the ceiling and then back at his father. It wasn't exactly an eye-roll, but his mother took it as one. She stood up.

"Don't you dare make this about you, Justin," she said. "This isn't about your resentment toward us. This is about your father and what's he's been through today."

"I know that! I was just—" He sighed and threw up his hands.

"You were trying to help." His father's voice was quiet, without a trace of fight in it.

Justin nodded. "Yeah. That's it. I was trying to help."

His mother stood still, looking from one to the other.

"Sit down, Rachel," said Justin's dad.

For another minute she stared at each of them, then she sat down and gave Justin a half-smile. "I'm sorry. I thought—I guess I'm more upset about this than I realized."

"It's been one wreck of a night," Justin agreed.

The fire that usually rose in him during an altercation with his parents was gone. He felt empty, chilled. Suddenly he didn't want to have secrets from them—not anymore. Sure, it was exciting at first, but it ate away at him until he was a ball of raw nerves, ready to fight with anyone who gave him half a reason.

*I'm sick of fighting.*

And then there was Savannah. He was starting to think that what he had pegged for distraction and shyness was really something else, something deeper. The idea scared him, because it made him feel somehow responsible for her and even more guilty for taking her out to Merrillee Road.

*I can't keep doing this. Can't keep sneaking and lying and pretending.*

But what would his parents think of him when he told them what he really did online every night? Would they kick him out?

He looked at his dad, who was staring at the carpet, shoulders slumped. Maybe it wasn't the best time to tell his father, but if he didn't do it now, the chance—and the courage—might not come again.

Justin cleared his throat. "While we're all here and miserable," he said, "there are some things I need to tell you guys."

His father looked up at him and said, "Thank God."

Justin frowned, confused.

"We know you've been struggling, son," said his father. "I've been praying that you would be open with us about it."

For a moment Justin thought of rebelling, backing out, pretending that he really had nothing to confess. But his relief at his dad's reaction overcame the impulse.

He nodded. "It's about time I told you. I need help."

His mother stood up again, and Justin and his dad looked at her, waiting for an outburst.

# The Silent

But she smiled. "Don't be so jumpy. I'm going to make hot chocolate. We might as well be comfortable while we bare our souls."

She left the room, and Justin's dad grinned. "Your mom's a great woman."

"Yeah," said Justin. "Not perfect—but great."

# 16

## Shadow of Fear

### Nikki's Digital Diary
<Posted Thursday, October 20, 9:05 p.m.>

I'm not ready to believe that all my blog-monitoring has gone to waste. After all, Savannah is a troubled girl, and just because she is dating Justin doesn't mean that she isn't capable of doing something desperate. So today I watched for her.

When Savannah came into our first class, she went straight to her seat without speaking or looking at anyone. Her face was a couple shades paler than it had been yesterday, and she looked thinner, which frightened me a little.

I dreaded the lunch hour, since it would mean facing—or avoiding—Haley and Justin. At noon I saw Haley walking ahead of me toward the cafeteria. I felt angry and a little sick. Being mad at your best friend is definitely not good for the appetite. The moment I walked in, I saw Justin already in the food line.

I had sent Haley an email about Justin. She had not responded, but I knew she would be just as angry with him as with me. So where would we all sit today?

# The Silent

Justin was nearing the end of the line. I figured he would find a spot with some other guys, and Haley would find her own spot, and that would be the end of the Prayer Table.

But Haley moved to the end of the line and touched Justin's arm. She was frowning as she spoke to him. I wondered what she was saying.

After a moment, Justin nodded. He went to an empty table and set down his tray.

Haley came back along the line. As she passed me, she said, "Sit with him when you get through. The three of us need to talk."

I didn't like being ordered around, but she was right. When I had gotten my food, I sat down next to Justin. In spite of being disappointed in him, I couldn't help admiring his profile as he stared at his food.

Haley joined us in a few minutes, closed her eyes, and said, "Dear Lord, thank you for this food. Please help us all to work out our differences and stay friends. Amen."

She opened her eyes again and stared at each of us. "Okay. We have problems."

"I'm sorry," said Justin.

I raised my eyebrows.

Haley frowned. "Well, I expected that to be longer in coming."

"I had kind of a wake-up call last night," he said. "I've been really frustrated lately. Feeling trapped, you know? And I've been putting stuff in my head that I shouldn't. But I told my parents about it, and they're going to help me. They forgive me, but I really want forgiveness from you guys too."

"We forgive you," I said.

"Yeah, of course," said Haley.

Justin looked straight at me, and I blushed.

"Nikki, I'm especially sorry for what I said about you last night."

"No, you were right. It looked pretty stalker-ish," I said. "But there's something else going on with me. Something that's so important it has distracted me from other important things, like my friends."

I glanced at Haley. "It's something I haven't told anyone, not even my dad. And you guys have to keep it a secret, okay?"

They nodded, and I told them about Kaye Daulton and her investigation, about the pictures in the restroom and the Garden of Lost Souls.

"That's why I was following you," I said. "I had just learned that Savannah is TheFourthFate."

"She might be TheFourthFate, but she wouldn't hurt anyone," said Justin. "She seems kind of . . . breakable."

"And you thought taking her out to Merrillee Road would be good for her?" said Haley.

Justin rolled his eyes. "Hey, I never claimed to be the world's smartest guy."

"So what do we do?" asked Haley.

"You two do nothing," I said. "I'll keep watching her."

"We can help watch," said Haley.

"Okay, but no questions."

"Agreed," said Justin. He put his hand in the center of the table, and Haley and I laid ours on top of it. It felt so right to laugh together again.

"So we're good?" I asked Haley.

She grinned. "We're good."

I took a deep breath and picked up my barbecue sandwich.

Sitting in social studies that afternoon, I watched the students file in. But I did not see Savannah.

When the bell rang, I glanced at Haley. She shrugged.

Five minutes into the lecture, still no Savannah.

I tried not to worry, but I couldn't shake the sense that something was wrong. At last I excused myself for a restroom break and slipped out into the hall.

The first place to check was the nurse's station. If Savannah had gone home sick, the nurse would know.

# The Silent

I hurried to the room and found the nurse standing beside Bob Milburn, who was gripping his inhaler and desperately sucking in breath. I waited till his breathing eased before stepping forward.

"Ms. Addison, have you seen Savannah recently?" I asked. "She didn't come to class, and I wondered if she was sick."

"Ah, yes," said the nurse. "She came in here a short while ago feeling sick to her stomach. I told her to wait till I finished with Bob. I guess she left."

I went back into the hall, more concerned than before. Why hadn't Savannah returned to class after leaving the nurse's station? Had she passed out somewhere? I decided to check the bathrooms.

The girls' bathroom next to the gym was rarely used during class periods because it was so far away from most of the classrooms. It would be empty at this time of day, the perfect place to go if you were feeling sick and miserable.

When I entered the bathroom, I heard someone retching in one of the stalls.

"Savannah?" I tried to open the door. Of course it was locked.

I heard her sigh, and a second later she collapsed onto the floor.

"Savannah!"

She did not answer.

This wasn't the time to be squeamish. The space between the stall partitions and the floor was wide enough for me to crawl through, so I stepped into the next stall and wormed into Savannah's. She lay on the floor, her face whiter than the tiles.

I unlocked the stall door, stepped over her, and ran back to the nurse's station.

"Savannah is in the gym bathroom!" I said. "She passed out."

The nurse grabbed her cell phone and her bag and ran with me to the bathroom. Savannah was still unconscious.

Seconds later, the principal arrived, puffing heavily.

"Is the girl hurt?" he asked.

"She passed out," I said.

He pushed past me to speak to the nurse.

When the paramedics arrived, they sent me out of the bathroom. I sat in the hall and watched them carry Savannah away. The principal followed, wiping his forehead with a paper towel. He would have to deal with Savannah's parents once he reached the hospital, and I suspected he was more worried about lawsuits and falling enrollment than about Savannah's health.

The nurse returned to her station to check on Bobby. I tagged along.

"Will she be all right?" I asked.

"I think so," said the nurse. "But she's definitely dehydrated. She probably has a virus. A severe one if I'm not mistaken. "

She opened the door to her station. Bobby's color was much better now; he was texting on his cell phone.

She turned back to me. "You can go back to class now, Nikki. Do you need a note?"

"Probably."

"And don't spread this around among your friends, okay? I'm sure the principal will want to communicate this himself."

She wrote me a note, and I handed it to Mrs. Mawley when I returned to class. Haley wouldn't stop staring; I knew she was dying of curiosity. I felt my cell phone vibrate in my pocket. She probably considered this enough of an emergency to break the no-texting-in-class rule. But there were only a few minutes of the period left. She could wait.

The instant the bell rang, she was at my desk. "So?"

I closed my notebook and got up. "So it looks like I'll be needing the lecture notes from you."

"Stop being so secretive, Nikki," she said as we headed out the door. "What happened? Why were you gone so long?"

"You can't tell anyone."

"Of course not."

In a whisper I told her about Savannah.

"Oh my goodness!" she said. "Is she all right?"

# The Silent

"They aren't sure what's wrong with her yet, but the nurse says she'll probably be okay."

Haley's eyes grew wider, and she grabbed my arm. "Nikki," she whispered. "What if it's the Silent?"

My heart flipped over. "What do you mean?"

"Well, it could be some kind of drug, or virus."

"Like a terrorist thing?"

"Maybe."

I glanced down the hall. It seemed gloomy in spite of the bright ceiling lights and colorful book bags.

"Someone could do something to our water or our food," said Haley. "And we wouldn't know until—"

"Stop it!" I said. "Just stop. You're freaking me out."

"Sorry."

As we continued down the hall, I eyed the water fountain. Ray Veres stepped up, pushed the button on the side, and put his mouth to the arc of water. I wanted to say, "Don't drink!" but I didn't want to cause a false alarm about poisoned water. I had no proof of that, just a theory from Haley's overactive imagination . . .

---

I was anxious about the possibility of a Silent before, but now I'm afraid. Haley's comment has made the danger real to me. And I don't think I want to investigate anymore. In fact, I don't even know if I want to go to school tomorrow.

Maybe I'll call Kaye tomorrow and tell her that I won't be her eyes and ears anymore. I'll tell her that I quit. She shouldn't be depending on a high school girl like me to catch the Silent for her. It's too much pressure.

# 17

## Tears

### Nikki's Digital Diary
<Posted Friday, October 21, 10:00 p.m.>

Today was busier than a Friday should be. I called Kaye in the morning, and after school I went to see Savannah. Neither conversation turned out as I expected it would.

---

Kaye was at home when I called, probably selecting another perfectly pressed suit from her closet. I could hear the faint metallic swish of clothes being moved along a closet rod.

"What's new, Nikki?" she said.

I told her about Savannah. Then I told her what Haley had said.

"This is no joke," I said. "It's real. What if somebody did make Savannah sick on purpose? Any of us could be next. I could be next."

"I heard about your classmate," said Kaye. "I already called the hospital, and they said it's just the flu. A serious case, but she should be okay. It just hit her hard because she hasn't been eating well."

"That's not my point," I said. "What if it hadn't been the flu? I mean, you're the detective. Shouldn't you be doing something more to catch this Silent? Instead of relying on me for information?"

My right hand and the cell phone in it were shaking. I brought up my left hand to steady it.

"Nikki, I understand that you're scared," said Kaye. "Believe me, I am doing all that I can from my end. I've been receiving regular reports from your principal, the teachers, and the school counselor. They are keeping a close eye on the problem students."

"But you said that the problem students aren't always the dangerous ones."

"Nikki, take a deep breath."

I sucked in a lungful of air and let it out again.

"Feel better?" Kaye asked.

"A little."

"Okay. I'm going to tell you something that's a little scary, but it's the truth. And I think you're woman enough to handle it."

"Okay." I prayed that she was right. At the moment I didn't feel *woman enough* to handle the bus ride.

"Nikki, the truth is that no matter what we do, someone could attack the student body at Mourning High. Someone could fool us into thinking he is harmless, while he's really deadly. But trust me when I tell you that my job, and the job of the entire Mourning Police Department, is to protect you and your fellow students from any kind of harm. And we take that responsibility very seriously. Do you understand?"

"Yes."

"I didn't ask for your help so that I could spare myself some work. I'm not sitting over here with my heels on my desk, drinking lattes."

I had to smile. The image of Kaye with her heels on the desk and her chair tilted back was too funny. "I know. I didn't mean to offend you."

"I know that. I just want to make sure you know that we are doing everything possible to find the person who was cruel enough to send those emails. Any information you can give me is icing on the cake, not the cake itself."

I took another deep breath. "Thanks."

"You're welcome. Now get your things together and head to school, and don't worry. I'll come down there this morning and sample the water myself."

After ending the call, I got up and gathered the books I would need for the day. Just before my second period class, I saw Principal Rudie and Kaye walking away from me toward the gym wing. Seeing her there, keeping us safe, made me feel nearly myself again.

After school Haley went home to baby-sit the Porc, and Dad took me to see Savannah at the Mourning hospital.

She lay still and silent under sheets not much whiter than her face. I wondered if her mom's health insurance would cover the bills. Hospital stays are insanely expensive.

"Hey, Savannah," I said, moving to the side of the bed. "How're you doing?"

Her skin looked almost transparent. I wondered if stomach flu was the only thing wrong with her.

"Are you okay?" I said. "You look pretty weak."

"Yeah. The doctor says that I have a virus, and I'm underweight. I guess I have a ways to travel before I can get back to normal life."

"Ah, yes. Wonderful normal life," I said.

A smile flickered over her face, and I knew she sensed the irony too. "Nothing like a hospital to make you appreciate your own bedroom."

I sat down in the chair near the bed.

"So, do you have a pastor or a priest here in town?" I asked, though I already knew the answer.

She shook her head.

"Well, there's this couple I know—he's not exactly a pastor, but he and his wife are really good people. Really wise about life, you know. Would you like me to have him come see you?"

She stared at me.

"They won't pry into your life," I said. "Not unless you want them to. But they're good at encouraging people in trouble."

"And you're not?"

I felt my face flush. "I'm not experienced with—I mean, I'm just a kid. I'm not really good at giving advice."

She shrugged. "I'm not into shrinks or counselors. They don't really care. They look at you like you're just an interesting case instead of a person. And they tell other people about you afterwards, over dinner, or when they're giving a lecture."

I knew she was right about the last part. I had heard preachers tell stories from the pulpit about people they had counseled. They called them "illustrations." The pastor usually gave the person in the story a fake name like "John" or "Mary" so that no one would be able to trace the tale back to its source. But I always felt guilty listening to those stories, as if I were peering into a room with "Do Not Disturb" on the door.

"I know what you mean," I told Savannah. And then the words that I had vowed not to say popped out. "I read your blog."

"My blog?"

"The Garden of Lost Souls. You're TheFourthFate, aren't you?"

She sighed and closed her eyes. "How did you know it was me?"

"The red book bag with the yellow teddy bear key chain."

"How long have you known?"

"I found out on Wednesday."

"Is that why you followed Justin and me that night?"

"Sort of. I didn't know that it was Justin picking you up. I thought you might be involved in something else."

She opened her eyes. "Like what?"

I didn't see any way around her question, so I said, "Like the threats on the school."

She chuckled hoarsely. "Don't make me laugh. It hurts."

"I'm not kidding."

"What are you? A private investigator?"

"No. But I wasn't following you because I was jealous."

"It wouldn't have mattered to me if you were," said Savannah. "I don't really care about Justin. He was just a guy who asked me out."

"Why did you go out with him if you didn't care?" I asked.

She stared at the wall behind me. "I wanted to feel something. It was all so empty. But Justin made me feel pretty. Like I was some one worth wanting."

I wanted to tell her why it was wrong to think like that, but before I could form the words, the nurse stepped in. "Time to go, Miss Altemann."

I stood up. "I'll come back soon, if you want."

Savannah nodded.

As I rode downstairs in the elevator, I thought about what I would have said if I had had more time. "Your worth as a human being doesn't depend on another person. It depends on you, and on the Person who made you. Don't rely on someone else to make you feel special."

Mom's face came into my mind before I could stop it, and my eyes watered. Since I was alone, I let myself cry a little before the elevator stopped to pick up another person. The hospital assistant who got in glanced at my weepy eyes, pushed the button for the ground floor, and stared at the doors until we touched ground again. When the doors opened, she strode out without a word or a glance.

I stepped into the hospital lobby, wondering what had made her so unsympathetic. She probably saw tear-stained faces every day of her life. Maybe she had become immune to them. Maybe that was the only way she could deal with the constant stress and anguish of the people all around her. The pain wasn't even hers. Why should she have to carry it?

*Why should I have to carry it?*

Maybe I should try not caring about people for a while. Just to see how it felt.

As I crossed the lobby, I saw a middle-aged woman standing beside an old man with a walker. The man took tiny shuffling steps, moving so slowly that his companion became irritated. Her face grew redder by the second.

"Dad, I'm going to run ahead and talk to the nurse over there," she said at last. "Just keep moving toward the elevator, okay?"

The man was so focused on walking that he did not answer. His daughter whisked away to the information desk, leaving him to shuffle on alone.

I felt a stab of pity for him, mixed with a twinge of fear. I could not imagine ever being like that, so wrinkled and weary that walking twenty feet was a major accomplishment. But someday, light years from now, I might be behind a walker just like that.

Now, if ever, was a moment to practice not caring. Deliberately I looked away from the old man and walked out through the rotating doors of the hospital. Dad stood beside one of the huge concrete planters out front, talking on his cell phone. As I waited beside him, I pictured myself ignoring the old man, placing the first layer of indifference over my heart. Like a callous from a cramped shoe, that layer would grow thicker and thicker until all the pumice stones and foot soaks in the world could not peel it off.

It was a disgusting image. Of course I didn't want my heart to be deadened like that.

It's like Mrs. Land said. You shouldn't stop caring just because it hurts. That's what love is. The greatest stories in the world are about people who sacrificed something precious for what they loved.

Loving other people, caring about their needs and their problems, is like dying a little bit for everyone.

---

In that moment, I think I got a better picture of what it was like for Christ to live on earth before His death. I have always pictured Him as being sad and solemn most of the time, and now I understand why. It's because He saw and heard and carried more of other people's pain than anybody else ever could.

# 18

## Seeing Blue

---

### Nikki's Digital Diary
<Posted Saturday, October 22, 9:15 p.m.>

This afternoon before dinner, while I was doing homework, I heard a car drive up. When no one rang the doorbell, I got up and went to my bedroom window to see who it was.

---

A man was leaning against a black pickup, texting on his cell phone. I recognized the guy from the bar the other night—the one who had offered to drive Tae home.

Instantly I was furious. I ran downstairs and out the side door.

"I thought I told you to stay away from here," I said, walking up to him.

"Ah, it's the protective little sister," he said.

"That's right," I said. "What are you doing here?"

"Tae owes me. I'm just here to collect. I don't want trouble."

Now that I saw him in daylight, I liked him even less. I didn't like the look in his eyes or the way the right corner of his mouth curved up in a perpetual smirk.

"How much does he owe you?" I asked.

"That's between him and me."

# The Silent

"If my dad comes home and finds you here, it's not going to stay between him and you."

He snapped his phone shut. "Then why don't you get upstairs and drag your brother out here? Then I'll leave."

I glared at him for a moment before going inside.

"Tae," I called. "Some guy's here to see you."

He didn't answer when I knocked on his door. No wonder. The volume of the music inside threatened to shake the walls down.

I pounded harder. "Tae? If you don't open up, I'm coming in!"

The music faded suddenly, and a minute later, Tae opened the door. "What is it?"

"You look terrible again," I said, staring at his wrinkled clothes and unshaven face. "I thought you were going all clean and professional. Phew! Have you showered lately?"

"None of your business." He wiped his face on the sleeve of his T-shirt. "Did you have a reason for banging on my door?"

"Yeah. There's a guy in the driveway that says you owe him money."

"What?" He looked startled. "What does he look like?"

"Dark hair, thin, but pretty buff, and he has this annoying half-smile."

"Casey." Tae's eyes narrowed. "Thinks he can fool me, the idiot. I don't owe him a cent."

"He seems pretty sure of it," I said. "Did you gamble that night, when you were drunk?"

"No. I'm telling you, I don't owe him money!"

I hesitated. "He never actually said it was money. He just said you owed him. Could it be something else?"

My brother's face tightened. "It could be. He did me a favor once; maybe he wants one in return."

"Like what kind of favor?"

"You don't need to know." He walked past me towards the stairs.

"Taylor!" I grabbed his sleeve. "He's bad news. I can tell. Maybe you should call Dad."

"No, thanks."

"Then maybe I'll call him."

He turned on me, his eyes burning. I backed up a step. For the first time since we were both in grade school, I was afraid he might hit me.

As I stared into his eyes, I saw that under the anger was fear—hollow, desperate fear.

"Let me help you," I said.

He shook his head. "I don't want to get you involved."

The front door opened and closed. Tae and I froze, listening. Was it Dad?

"Anyone home?" Casey's voice echoed through the house.

"He can't just walk in here!" I whispered, shocked.

Tae grabbed my arm and pushed me toward my room. "Go in your room and stay there, Nikki. Let me handle this."

I decided it would be wise to obey him, at least for the moment, so I went into my room and shut the door. But the minute I heard his feet reach the bottom of the stairs, I slipped out of my room and crept into the bathroom. There was a vent in the floor there that acted sort of like a voice conductor. If Tae and Casey spoke near the vent in the ceiling of the downstairs hall, I would be able to hear most of what they said.

It was eavesdropping, plain and simple, but I told myself I was doing it to protect my brother. Besides, it seemed like a natural extension of all the eavesdropping and investigating I had been doing at school.

"What do you want, Casey?" Tae's voice, thin and metallic, echoed up through the vent.

"Payback, brother," said Casey. "I've had news that the police may be sniffing around my place soon. I need you to hold onto a few things for me until it all blows over."

"You want me to keep the stuff here for you? Do you know what my dad would do to me if he found out?"

"That's the price of living at home, partner," said Casey. "You'll have to weigh the risk. What would make him more angry—finding my stash, or finding out why you owe me one?"

Tae answered with a curse, and I winced. He never said those words when Dad was around.

"Your little sister is quite a looker," said Casey. "Real spunky too. She told me to leave you alone, or else."

My face grew hot.

"She's got nothing to do with you. She's just a kid."

"A kid? She's what—sixteen? Seventeen?"

Tae's voice was so low I could barely make out the words. "You really don't want to go there."

Casey laughed. "All right, man. Have it your way. We'll keep this strictly business."

"I'm not hiding your stuff here."

"I'll give you a cut after it's sold."

There was silence, and I knew Tae was considering the offer. *No!* I pleaded silently. *Don't do it! It's not worth it.*

"Times are hard for everyone, bro," said Casey. "A dude's got to make a living somehow. What do you say?"

I did not want to hear what Tae would say. I stood up and crept back to my room, where I dialed Kaye's number on my cell.

She picked up on the second ring. "Nikki?"

"Kaye! I need your help. There's a guy at my house—his name is Casey. He told my brother that the police might be sniffing around his place soon, and he's trying to get my brother to agree to store here whatever they're sniffing for until everything blows over. My brother doesn't want to do it."

"Casey is his first name?"

"Yes. I don't have a last name. He's probably in his early twenties, dark hair, thin, maybe a little taller than six feet."

"I think I know who he is. He's probably hiding drugs or guns. I'll do some checking with a colleague of mine. If they're already planning a raid on Casey's house, maybe we can speed things up—get to the stuff before he has a chance to move it. No guarantees, though. I need probable cause before acting on something like this. Just keep your brother from getting involved, okay? I can't cover for him."

"I know," I said. "Thanks!"

"Nikki? Don't let anyone know that you spoke with me. The kid might start thinking about revenge on the person who turned him in."

"I understand."

I closed my phone and tucked it into my book bag. A few minutes later the front door slammed and the black pickup's engine growled. I hurried to the window.

Tae was in the passenger seat.

"Oh, no! No!"

I raced downstairs, out the front door, and down the driveway. I waved frantically at the departing pickup as it turned the corner and slid out of sight.

Too late. Tae had gone with Casey. Now he would be arrested too, as an accomplice or accessory of some kind. The word "accessory" made me think of earrings and purses and belts. That's what Tae would be—an earring on somebody else's crime.

I stood in the driveway in my bare feet, watching the brown leaves scuttle across the pavement. The autumn breeze felt suddenly cold.

A minute later the black pickup reappeared around the corner, heading for our house. I gasped with relief. Tae must have seen me waving and asked Casey to turn around.

My brother leaned out the passenger side window, looking incensed. "What's wrong with you?"

The lie leaped off my tongue before I had a chance to think. "Dad's on the house phone," I said. "He wants to talk to you."

"Did you tell him anything?"

"No," I said.

Tae turned to Casey. "Gotta go. My dad's on the phone."

Casey was staring at me, straight into my eyes. I wished he would stop, but I didn't dare glance away, or he might know I had lied.

"You go talk to him," he said to Tae. "I'll wait for you here."

"What if he's heading home?" said Tae.

"Fine," said Casey, still staring at me. "I'll call you, man. And you'd better pick up the phone when I do."

"I will." Tae opened the truck door and hopped out. "Come on, sis."

We jogged toward the house. Once we were both inside, I closed the door and turned both locks.

Tae went into the kitchen, and I followed. The phone sat silent in its cradle on the counter.

Tae pointed to it. "You hung up on him?"

"No," I said.

He frowned.

"I lied. Dad didn't call."

"You lied to me?"

"I'm sorry. It happened so fast. I couldn't think of what to say. I didn't want you to leave again."

"Isn't lying a cardinal sin for you or something?" he said. "Christians don't lie, right?"

"They aren't perfect either." Inside I felt like crying. With that one little lie, I had damaged my brother's view of what it meant to be a Christian.

"I'm an adult," said Tae. "I can go out with my friends if I want to."

"Yes," I said, looking him in the eye. "You're an adult. You make your own choices."

He tilted his head to one side. "You were listening, weren't you? The bathroom vent?"

I looked away.

"That's a childish thing to do, Nik."

"You're not yourself, Tae. I didn't want you to have to handle this alone."

"But I am alone!" The sudden volume of his voice startled me. "Mom's gone. Dad's never here. Most of my friends are in college somewhere, not stuck in this crummy town. I am nothing. I have nothing! I have no future, no plan for my life. I have no skills and no motivation to learn any skills. I can't even get a job flipping burgers!"

He was leaning against the wall, breathing hard. The look in his eyes scared me. His right hand hung loose at his side, so I took it carefully in my own.

"Come on," I said. "Let's sit down."

We sat on the couch in silence for several minutes. I wanted to talk, to try and pull his emotions out of him. But somehow I managed to sit quietly, and wait, and listen.

At last he began to speak.

"I don't have to tell you everything, and I'm not going to," he said. "Casey did cover for me once when I did something stupid. End of story. Now he expects me to pay him back. But I guess you already heard about that."

"Kind of." I made him my best apology face.

He sighed. "I feel really useless these days. Like, what's the point of living, you know? Life is just more trouble than it's worth."

"You don't mean that," I said. "You're just feeling down because you don't have a job yet, and because of college, and because of Mom."

"Right." He sighed again. "You know what scares me, Nikki? That stuff that Casey's into—I could get into that. I could be good at it; I could make more money than I ever could working any of the little entry-level jobs in this town. It would be really easy to go that way. And why shouldn't I, after all?"

"Because it's wrong," I said. "You'd be hurting people."

"They wouldn't have to buy the stuff if they didn't want to," he said.

"But it would be illegal."

He shrugged. "And part of me doesn't care."

The Silent

"Sin is attractive to all of us," I said. "But when you trust God, He gives you the strength to resist it."

"Like you did just now, with your lie."

"I'm not perfect. Believe me, I feel guilty about lying to you. When I sin, I feel so bad that I have to ask God's forgiveness and the forgiveness of the person I hurt. We're all sinners. But when Christ comes into your life, He makes you holy before God, and He helps you want to do right."

Tae leaned back and clasped his hands behind his head. He looked as though he were trying to form his thoughts into words.

"I watch a lot of fantasy movies, and I play a lot of video games," he said. "In those story lines, you sometimes have a character that was good once, until they were corrupted by some evil spirit. All their friends have to do is kick the evil spirit out, and their pal is good again. This isn't one of those games, Nikki. This is real life. You can't just banish the evil in someone and turn them good. I wish it were true, but my head tells me it's not."

"It is true," I said. "I'm not going to preach at you, Tae. But I think you should read a little bit of the Bible—the Gospel of Mark especially. I think you'll be surprised at some of the stories in there."

"Anything about evil spirits?"

"Actually, yes." I grinned at his surprise. "Check it out."

"I don't have a Bible."

"You can use mine. Or you can read it online."

"Maybe."

I knew that if I pushed him too hard, I would lose the ground I had gained; so I stood up. "I'm going to do some homework before Dad gets home," I said. "Catch you later."

"Later," said Tae.

---

I'm encouraged, even hopeful. I wasn't able to tell Tae much about Christ, but God can grow those little bits of truth into something more powerful—in spite of my own imperfectness getting in the way.

# 19

## Savannah

**In Savannah Mason's room at
Mourning General Hospital**

Savannah lay statue-still in her hospital bed, thinking.

Maybe in some far-off exotic place, life had meaning. But the world Savannah lived in was small and dark. It consisted of just a few changes of scenery. There was her room, the bathroom, and the kitchen at home; and at school there were the classrooms, the lunch room, the library, and the bathrooms. Sometimes there was gym or detention or a trip to the mall with her mom.

And now there was the hospital, a building full of people in pain. The nurses watched her all day and all night. They treated her like something breakable.

She tried not to think back to that magical summer at her dad's villa in Florida, when she and Kai had roamed the beaches and boardwalks and malls together. The days had been so hot and color-ful, and the nights softly gloomy and twinkling with a thousand stars. She tried not to remember the ripple of Kai's laughter, the sun turning his hair golden, and the drops of water sparkling on his brown skin.

It had been the best two months of her life.

# The Silent

When she came back to Mourning, she had tried to hold on to the shreds of it. She looked at the hundreds of photos she and Kai had taken together—looked at them for hours and hours. She dressed in the same outfits she had worn in Florida, until the weather became so cold that even her mother noticed her skimpy clothes and yelled at her to put a jacket on.

At last, after a thousand attempts to contact Kai and a million excuses for why he wasn't responding, she was forced to accept the truth. She had been nothing to him but a summer girlfriend—someone to hang out with and laugh with and even pretend to love. For him, it was over from the moment they said their last tearful goodbye in the driveway of her dad's house. All the promises of emails and text messages and future visits were as empty as the shells they had gathered on the beach.

Around and around the circle went, day after day of the same faces, the same desks, the same blank hallways, and the same rotation of meals in the cafeteria. At home Savannah had to eat, drink, do homework, and sleep. She blogged now and then, when the anguish became too strong to hold inside.

And then the Christian boy, Justin, had asked her out. Dimly she had hoped that he might have some answers. But it turned out that he was also disillusioned with his world.

When Justin brought her home that night after the run-in with Nikki Altemann, Savannah had tried to sneak downstairs to her basement bedroom without her mother noticing. But a shrill voice from the kitchen stopped her short.

"Savannah?"

She closed her eyes and sighed. Mom was home, and not watching TV, which meant she was in one of her critical moods.

When Savannah stepped into the kitchen, her mother stared. "Those are some short shorts."

"Sorry." Savannah tugged at the hems.

"Why are your legs so skinny?" said her mother. "They look like little sticks. You need some flesh on those gams, my girl. Have a snack." She gestured toward the fridge.

"How was your day?" said Savannah.

"Same old, same old. You know," said her mother.

Savannah nodded. "I know."

"Sit," said her mother. "Let's talk."

Savannah sat down across the table from her.

"So did you have a date or something?" her mother asked.

"Yes. His name's Justin."

"Pretty short date."

"Something came up."

Her mother raised an eyebrow and said, "Hmm." Then she picked up the newspaper and began reading the comics.

Savannah went to the freezer, took out a carton of Moose Tracks ice cream, and began to scoop some into a bowl.

"When I said, 'Get a snack,' I didn't mean ice cream," said her mother. "It'll give you pimples. And pimples on a pale face like yours look twice as bad. You know, you should get a tan. I had a great tan when I was your age."

Savannah had put the ice cream back in the freezer, gone to her room, and sat on the bed, descending into the familiar black tunnel of depression.

"Savannah?" A nurse smiled at her from the doorway, breaking her reverie. "Someone's here to see you."

Her mother had promised to visit since it was Sunday afternoon and she did not have to work, so Savannah was surprised to see Nikki Altemann's face over the nurse's shoulder. She was holding a big yellow sunflower.

"Can I come in?" asked Nikki.

Savannah nodded. "Yeah."

She had not expected Nikki to visit her even once, but she had. And here she was again for a second time. Savannah wasn't sure she liked Nikki, but she did not hate her either. She had no energy for that.

Whatever Nikki's motives were, she had at least seemed genuine—willing to help, but not annoyingly so.

# The Silent

"So . . . how's it going?" said Nikki, sitting down and rubbing both hands on her jeans.

Oddly, Nikki's nervousness made Savannah feel more comfortable. "I'm doing better. I'll be able to get out of here soon."

"Good."

*Here it comes*, thought Savannah. *The awkward silence.*

It lasted for a minute or so. Then Savannah asked, "So what's new at school? Anything interesting?"

"Not really," said Nikki. "Claire and Jason got back together again. You know them, right?"

Savannah rolled her eyes. "Everybody knows them. They've had more break-ups and gotten back together more times than any other couple in the state."

"They're a roller coaster, for sure."

Nikki talked for several minutes about school gossip and homework. Savannah watched her. Before the encounter on Merrillee Road, she had hardly ever thought about Nikki; and when she did, she thought of her as "the perfect girl," the one who never did anything wrong, always achieved good grades, and had no family problems. But then there had been that news about Nikki's parents breaking up.

She wondered how Nikki was coping. She seemed stable and collected, but was that just a mask? Savannah knew all about putting on a good show for the world. Everyone wanted to think that you were okay, even if you were bleeding inside. They didn't really want to be bothered with your problems. It was best to pretend that everything was fine.

"Savannah?"

Savannah looked up, suddenly conscious that Nikki had stopped talking several seconds ago.

"Are you okay?" said Nikki.

"I was thinking."

"What about?"

Savannah looked straight into her eyes. "Forget the school news. I want to hear about you. I've always thought that you had a perfect life, but you don't, do you?"

She saw tears sparkle in Nikki's eyes.

"No, I don't have a perfect life."

"Who does?" said Savannah.

"Right." Nikki laughed, pulling a tissue from her bag. "Who wants a perfect life anyway? Boring!"

"You sound like Justin. He sent me a card, you know—and a letter like a mile long. Handwritten too."

"He apologized?"

"Yeah. He wrote because he didn't think I would want to see him."

"Do you?"

Savannah shrugged. "Maybe. But I have to work through some stuff first. My life hasn't exactly been sunshine and roses lately."

"I'm sorry."

"Don't be." Savannah readjusted her pillow. "So tell me how you've been dealing, with your mom gone and all that."

She knew the question was blunt almost to the point of being rude, but Nikki didn't seem to notice. She talked, and Savannah talked. Nikki threw in Bible verses sometimes; they were oddly refreshing, like a breath of clean air in a stuffy room.

"Wow, I've been here an hour," said Nikki at last. "It was great talking to you."

"You too."

"I almost forgot. I brought you something." She pulled a book from her bag. "It's a Bible study—a pretty easy read. I thought you might want to look at it if you're bored or whatever."

"Thanks." Savannah took the book and turned it over. Apparently it was for depressed teenage girls. *Like me*, she thought, smiling wryly. But she was grateful. Maybe the book would have more of those "fresh air" verses.

# The Silent

"I'd better get going," said Nikki, rising from her chair. "Call me if you ever want to talk. I wrote my number on the back of the bookmark."

"Thanks."

Nikki was a step beyond the doorway when she turned back. "I just had a thought," she said. "Would you ever want to come over to my place for the weekend? After you get out, you know. We could hang out with Haley and play games and watch movies and eat junk food. If you want."

It sounded fun . . . and normal. Savannah smiled.

"I'd have to ask my mom," she said. "But that sounds great. Thanks."

"Cool." Nikki grinned. "I'll see you around then."

When she had gone, Savannah relaxed against her pillows. A weekend at Nikki's house wasn't a summer vacation in Florida, but it was something to look forward to.

# 20

## Facing the Music

### Nikki's Digital Diary
<Posted Wednesday, October 26, 2:20 a.m.>

---

There were police cars at school again this morning. Three of them.
And just when I thought things were going to settle down.

---

Haley scrunched up next to me, trying to see out the bus window. "Wow. I wonder what happened this time."

As we headed to class, I passed Kaye Daulton in the hallway. Neither of us spoke, but she caught my eye, and I knew I would be getting a phone call later.

No sooner had I sat down in my first class than my cell phone buzzed. I glanced at it under my desk so the teacher wouldn't see. It was a text from Kaye.

"Doesn't she know you have class?" Haley whispered.

I shrugged and read the message. *Come to PR's office now. Will fix with teacher l8r.*

Sighing, I raised my hand and excused myself. Haley waved to me as I left the classroom, and I rolled my eyes at her. If she were any more curious, she would be one of the Source's Info Addicts.

# The Silent

The principal wasn't in his office, but Kaye was waiting for me in his big leather chair.

"A detective for principal," I said. "I like it."

She smiled briefly, but I could tell that she was not in the mood for jokes. "Have a seat, Nikki."

I sat down.

"As you know, we were called in this morning. A dead cat was left in the principal's parking spot last night, and there was another one on the school steps."

"Ew."

"Definitely. They were both hit by cars. At different times, probably. One of them looked more decayed than the other. That means whoever did this collected some roadside carrion and brought it here."

"A prank?"

"That's what we thought, until Principal Rudie told us that on the day he received the email threats, he found a dead cat on his patio."

I got chills. Several of them.

"You're kidding."

"I wish I was." Kaye shook her head. "We're here to question all the potential problem students again, and we're broadening our definition of problem student."

"Am I included in that?"

"Not yet. But I'm afraid you can't help me with this anymore. The department is going to follow procedure, and if they can't find the perp, there will be nothing more they can do. This incident will be regarded as a practical joke. Case closed."

"They can't do that," I said. "There's somebody here that's really messed up. I know it."

"How do you know? Instinct? That doesn't fly in the real world, Nikki."

"But it's the police's job to take instinct and find proof, right?" I said.

"We're understaffed and underfunded," said Kaye. "We can't keep watching the school and neglecting other parts of town. This whole email scare looks to my superiors like a simple case of a teen getting high off other people's panic."

"But you don't agree."

"I don't, but I can't prove anything or do anything. I've been given some other cases—cases that will take up my time and attention."

I stared at her. "So that's it."

"That's it."

I was angry, but I knew that Kaye didn't deserve my anger. So I managed a nod. "I understand. Thanks for all you've done."

I stood up, and so did she. "Don't be discouraged, or scared," she said. "If there is someone dangerous in this school, he will show himself eventually. And when he does, we'll take care of it."

"Thanks."

At lunch, I told Haley and Justin what had happened.

"So someone left a dead cat on the school steps and another in the principal's parking spot," said Justin.

"Couldn't it have been two cats fighting?" said Haley. "Like maybe there was a girl cat they both wanted, and they fought, and one of them killed the other one. But maybe the girl cat secretly liked the dead cat, so she killed the other cat and ran away?"

I stared at her. "What are you talking about?"

Haley shrugged. "Just trying to think of an explanation other than the scary one."

"Yours was pretty scary," said Justin.

"There isn't any other explanation," I said. "Whether or not the person who did this is dangerous enough to hurt someone, they're still pretty sick. Anybody who collects carrion from the roadside is messed up."

Neither Haley nor Justin had anything to say to that.

Haley came home with me after school. We set up our homework and nail-painting stuff in the living room and put a tray of frozen pizza bagels in the oven.

"I have to run up and talk to Tae for a minute," I told Haley. "I'll be right back."

Tae's bedroom door was partly open, so I stepped inside. He was reorganizing his collection of games—as if putting everything in alphabetical order would make it fit better on the overstuffed shelves.

"Heard anything from Casey lately?" I said.

He jumped. "You could knock."

"Sorry."

"You could also be a little more tactful."

"Again, sorry." I hopped on his bed and crossed my legs, meditation-style.

"I didn't hear from Casey, but I heard about him," said Tae. "The police raided his apartment."

"Good thing you didn't get involved."

He looked at me over his shoulder. "Why do I get the feeling that you already knew about his arrest?"

I shrugged. "Imagination maybe?"

"No, it's not that." He turned to face me. "Nikki, I know you're feeling all independent with Mom gone, and you've done a great job of being your own woman, but there are some things that a seventeen-year-old girl needs to stay away from. And that includes anything involving Casey. I want you to forget him. Forget his name. Forget everything about him."

"I will if you will."

He hesitated, and a little jolt of fear struck through my heart. Was he still considering Casey's way of life? Selling drugs and whatever else creepy criminals sold?

But after a few seconds, he nodded. "It's a deal."

We shook on it. Then he said, "Did I hear Haley giggling earlier?"

"Yeah, we're doing a pizza, nails, and homework night. Dad said it was okay."

"He'll be home late again?"

I nodded. Dad is working extra hours to make up for the missing income from Mom. We only see him at breakfast and after he comes home at nine.

"I'm dropping off a few resumes tomorrow," said Tae.

I didn't know what to say, so I said, "Good."

I knew that Tae's chances of finding a job in Mourning were practically zero. It was only a matter of time before he realized that too and decided to move away. The thought of him alone in a strange city made me sick to my stomach. He wasn't ready to be on his own; he needed someone to hold him steady, keep him from sliding over to the dark side.

As I passed the kitchen on my way to the living room, the phone rang.

I stopped. Most people who knew us called the cell phone of the person they wanted to talk to. But Grandma always called the house phone.

The phone rang again.

"Nikki?" called Tae from upstairs.

"I'll get it!" I yelled. I picked up the phone on the third ring. "Hello?"

"Hello, Nikki. It's your grandma."

"Hi, Grandma. It's good to hear from you." I tried to keep the words back, but they popped out anyway. "It's been a while."

"Yes, well, a lot has been going on. I figured I'd give you kids some space."

Nice excuse. "Thanks."

She asked me a few questions about school, and about Dad and Justin. Then she came around to the topic I knew was foremost in her mind.

"Nikki, I wanted to talk to you about college."

"Yes, Grandma?"

"Did you get the packet I sent you?"

"Yes."

"And which ones are you considering?"

*Lord, help me not to be rude,* I prayed.

# The Silent

"Grandma, I'm not going to any of those colleges. They all look awesome, but I really want to attend a Christian college."

Silence.

"Grandma?"

"Nikki, you understand that your degree would mean far more if you attended a reputable school?"

"I think we have different definitions of *a reputable school*," I said.

"There is only one definition, Nikki. And I don't appreciate your attitude about this. I've offered to help with your college tuition. Maybe you don't realize what a large sum I have in mind."

"I do, Grandma, and I'm grateful. But I know where I want to attend."

"You're being very stubborn," said my grandmother. "Just like your father. Your mother has told me stories. I had hoped you would lean to the Rafton side of the family. We Raftons have always been open-minded thinkers."

*Sure, Grandma. You were never stubborn a day in your life.*

"I wish you would think for yourself, Nikki, instead of just following along with your dad's religion. It's very sad. He used to be so different. This religious phase of his just changed him completely. It was the worst thing that could have happened to your family."

The anger I had been holding back flared up.

"Never talk about my dad like that," I said. "At least he is sticking with his family and supporting them. That's more than I can say for your daughter."

And I hung up the phone. I was shaking all over. Never before had I spoken to my grandmother like that.

The oven timer beeped. I turned it off and took out the pizza bagels, trying to calm myself by taking deep breaths. I shoveled the bagels onto two plates and carried them to the living room.

When I came in, Haley gave me her searching look—the one that usually results in a heart-to-heart girl talk, complete with tears and followed by a shopping spree.

"What's wrong?" she said.

I sat down beside her on the floor, still feeling shaky. "I just yelled at my Grandma."

"Really? I didn't hear any yelling."

"Well, I didn't exactly yell, but I said some things." I bit into a pizza bagel. The sauce burned my tongue, so I put it down. "My life is just crazy right now. There's too much to worry about."

Haley set her plate aside. "Tell me about it."

"Well, there's the stuff at school."

"The threats and the dead cats." She nodded.

"And then there's my dad. He's working so hard. And Tae is trying to find a job, but there's nothing. I'm afraid he'll decide to move away."

Haley nodded again.

"And then there are people at school—Savannah, and Carlen, and Will, and Justin, and others. They all have problems, and they're all hurting. I never used to notice how much the people around me were hurting, until I started looking."

"And listening," said Haley.

"But I don't want to listen anymore," I told her. "I don't want to see, and I don't want to care. I have enough problems of my own without thinking about everyone else's. Haley, why does God let such terrible things happen to people our age? The other kids at school are young, but they already have all this baggage. It's not fair."

I closed my eyes, trying not to burst into tears.

"And what about me? I'm His child, right? Doesn't He think I have enough on me with the threats at school, and the fights with my parents, and the stress over college? No, He had to go and throw in a divorce, and my brother's issues, and the personal dramas of half a dozen other people. Is that fair?"

Haley opened her mouth to reply, but I cut in.

"And don't just say, 'Life isn't fair,' because I already know that. I've had enough adults say that to me. But just because life isn't fair, doesn't mean that it shouldn't be. And I want God to step in and make it fair. Now."

Even as I said the words, I knew how awful and rebellious they sounded. But Haley didn't flinch.

"Life isn't fair . . . but it's not God's fault," she said. "It's ours. We sin, and sin has consequences. Sometimes He lets those consequences get really bad, so we can see just how twisted we are and how messed up our world has become. And that helps us come back to Him."

I sat up and stared at her. Was this Haley? My friend Haley, the blonde who thought shopping could change the world? Yes, there she was—same round face and perfect teeth, the same sparkly blue eyes.

"Where did that come from?" I asked.

She flushed. "I do some thinking too, you know. I just don't usually talk about it."

"Maybe you should start talking about it more," I said. "That was a pretty wise thing to say. I think I should write it down."

She laughed, but I was only half-joking.

---

So I'm writing her words here in my blog. I don't want to forget them.

# 21

## The Silent

---

## In the basement of 511 Pine Knob Circle

Tomorrow would be the day.

He had chosen it primarily for its sinister reputation. He envisioned a Wikipedia article in his mind, entitled "The Mourning High School Halloween Massacre."

He never thought of his intended victims as his classmates. To him they were robots in a painted, mechanical world. They were blobs of dough in a cookie factory, being stamped and baked into a thousand identical shapes. They deserved their fate. For years they had treated him no better than a piece of furniture—existent and useful at times, but mostly ignored. Unloved.

He was the one whose jokes were always followed by silence. The one who was never chosen to lead anything or perform in anything. The one who steadily achieved a B in every class and neither worried nor dazzled his teachers.

He was the one who was never invited to parties or to the movies on Friday night. The one who was never offered a seat in the cafeteria, but always had to ask, "May I sit here?" until he finally decided that he'd rather sit alone. The one whom girls avoided, almost by instinct, although they would call him "a nice guy" to their friends if he was lucky enough to surface in the conversation.

Most human beings would have wilted in the blankness of such a life, or else found a way to change. He had changed—deeply and drastically.

And tomorrow was the day that he would step out of his present self and into a new reality.

He wondered how his father would feel, after it was over. Maybe he would be too drunk to notice.

Until recently, he had intended to carry out the whole thing himself—one soul rebelling against hypocrisy and tyranny. Then he had found an accomplice. The accomplice's fury was more recent and more shallow than his own, but it would serve the purpose.

The accomplice was expendable. He must never forget that. It was the way of things. In chess, the queen, though more important than the pawns, would sacrifice her life for the king. The sidekick might die, but the superhero never did.

The King. The Superhero. Those were his titles. Tomorrow he would break out of the mold and become what he was meant to be.

A legend.

# 22

## Halloween

I haven't written in a while.

It seems kind of pointless now. Everyone knows what happened at Mourning High School on Halloween.

But I like to finish what I start. So I'm going to write what I saw, what I heard, and what I was thinking that day—the day the nightmare came true.

Halloween, in my experience, usually varies between two types of weather. Either it's cold and rainy, so that the trick-or-treaters have to hide their costumes under ponchos and raincoats, or it's the kind of blue autumn day that makes you want to rake up a pile of leaves and jump in it.

Halloween this year was bright blue with just enough puffy grey clouds to remind the world that this was only a temporary hiatus in Mourning's rainy season. The breeze pinched at my cheeks when I went outside, and I hugged my puffy jacket close, wishing I had opted for the leather one.

Haley called me just before I got on the bus.

# The Silent

"I'm throwing up my guts today," she said.

"Yuck!" I said. "Thanks for sharing."

"A stomach flu. Can you believe it?" she said. "I haven't had a stomach flu since grade school."

I frowned. "Do you think somebody—"

"Do I think the Silent had anything to do with it?" she interrupted. "No. My mom has been through enough of these with me and the Porc to know a regular strain of stomach flu from any weird virus. Don't worry, Nikki, another eight hours of yuck and I'll be on the road to recovery."

"It's a crime to have to stay indoors on a day like this," I told her. "This is gorgeous weather for hiking."

"Yeah, or shopping."

I laughed. "You're impossible. Even when you're sick you're thinking about shopping."

"I like to buy things."

"Be glad your dad still has a job so you can afford to do that," I said.

"Yeah, I know."

I knew we were both thinking about Justin's dad. Justin's family would probably be moving to a larger city in a month or two. He would have to adjust to a new school, a new town, and a new church. And there would be new girls too. He would probably email me and Haley for a while. Then it would be a Facebook message now and then, and eventually we would become disconnected.

It was inevitable. And it was depressing, after years of crushing on him, to know that in a few months we would be separated, probably forever.

On the way to my first class, I passed Todd Kendall in the hallway.

"Hey, Nikki!" he said. "See you in social studies."

"Hey, Todd," I said, surprised. He actually looked awake—even excited. Maybe he had a hot date to go trick-or-treating with.

I saw Jasmine in the hall after first period. "Hey, girl," I said. "I read that poem on your blog the other day."

She flushed, glancing around as if she was afraid someone might hear. "It's not very good."

"I liked it."

"Well, thanks." She came a step closer. "Where's Haley today?"

"She's at home, sick with the flu," I said.

Jasmine nodded. "Tell her I hope she gets better soon."

"I will."

One of the boys from Jasmine's group came up and tugged on her book bag. "Come on, Jas. You're going to be late."

She waved and vanished into the crowd of students.

I went on to my next class. After that it would be lunchtime. Justin would be at the Prayer Table. I'm trying only to care about him as a friend, especially after the problem with him and Savannah. Maybe their tryst was a sign of a deeper problem with his character. But I figure that everyone makes mistakes and learns from them, and if we didn't forgive each other, the world would be unlivable.

Jon and Arisha joined Justin and me for lunch.

"How's your dad's job hunt going?" asked Arisha.

"Pretty well. He's got a lead in Albany and another in Baltimore."

I frowned at my pizza. Albany was good—only a few hours away—but Baltimore? He might as well be going to California.

"He's thinking the one in Nashville might suit him better," said Justin. "Plus we have family there. My uncle Josh and his wife. You remember them, Nikki?"

"What? Oh yeah. I remember."

Josh and his wife Ginny had come up once for Christmas, two years ago. I hadn't liked him at all. At our Christmas banquet at the Berkell's, he had pulled my hair and teased me about boys in front of everyone, just to see me blush. Justin loved him, of course.

"Yeah, I've been to Baltimore a couple times," Justin continued. "I like it. Of course it'll take some getting used to, but hey—a new city, new places to go. What's not to love?"

I put down my half-eaten pizza.

"What's wrong, Nikki?" asked Arisha. "You are not feeling well?"

"Oh, no," said Justin, scooting his chair away a few inches. "Are you getting that stomach flu thing that Haley has?"

"No," I said. "I'm just not hungry."

"Nikki, not hungry for pizza?" said Jon. "That's got to be a first."

I managed to smile genuinely enough to fool them. Once the conversation moved back to Baltimore, I hid the leftover pizza under my napkin and picked up my tray.

"I have to stop by the library before class," I told the others. "Catch you later."

I didn't want to hear any more about Justin moving away, not because I wasn't interested in his family's future, but because it made his departure seem that much more real.

The Source and a few of his buddies were camped out on the benches by the library as usual. I waved to them as I passed. Micah grinned and waved back. Rob barely glanced at me, and he did not smile.

For some reason, the image of his unsmiling face stayed with me as I searched the library database for the book I wanted. Usually Rob wore a smile like mechanics wear utility belts. His grin was a part of him.

Had I offended him somehow? Though he wasn't exactly a friend, I liked Rob. I reviewed our email exchange in my mind and decided that nothing I said had been rude or cruel.

So what was his problem?

A hand touched my arm, and I jumped.

"Rob? You scared me!"

"Sorry."

Now that he stood before me, I saw that he looked more sober than angry. "Is something wrong?"

"It's the vibes. They're all wrong today."

I sighed and leaned back in the chair, trying to keep from smiling with relief. "You're getting bad vibes?"

"Yeah. I've had this feeling all day—like something bad is about to happen."

"Rob, it's Halloween," I said. "Lots of people have creepy-crawly feelings on this holiday. That's kind of what it's about, which is why I don't like it."

"I'm not talking about ghosts and long-nosed ghouls or whatever," he said. "I'm talking about *evil*."

The way he said it sent a chill down my spine. Suddenly I realized that, whatever I thought about the ridiculous term "vibes," Rob might actually be sensing a legitimate tension from someone near him. Maybe the Silent.

"When did you first feel these vibes?" I asked.

"I don't know. In my first class, I guess."

"Who sits near you in that class?"

"Eric Frese, Carlen Michaels, Todd Kendall, Luke Larabee—" He listed several more names. But my mind stopped after the first name.

Eric. Eric Frese.

Quiet, morose Eric, with his greasy black hair and those purple studs in his ears. He could be the Silent!

"Rob," I said. "Do you think that Eric might have sent those email threats?"

He shrugged. "What I want to know is why the police can't back trace the emails to a particular computer and nab the guy that way."

"They tried," I said. "The emails were sent from a library computer. Somebody didn't log out when they left, and whoever it was just took over, opened a new email account, and used that to send the threats, time-delayed to arrive Friday morning."

"That would be one way to do it. How do you know all that, anyway?" Rob sounded impressed. I had told him something that he, the Source, did not know.

"I have my sources," I said, smiling.

He chuckled. "Good ones too."

The admiration in his eyes embarrassed me, and I turned back to the search results on the screen before me.

"So what if it's Eric?" I said.

"There's one problem with that," said Rob. "Eric hates libraries. He never sets foot in them. And he is totally computer illiterate."

"Maybe that's a cover."

Rob looked unconvinced and a little nervous. Maybe I was taking his vibes too seriously and freaking him out.

I tried to lighten my tone. "Well, I'm sure it's not Eric then. I'm off to class. How about you?"

"No, I have a free period."

"Okay then. See you around."

He caught up with me before I reached the library doors. "Hey Nikki, you want to have lunch sometime?"

I froze, pondering all the reasons I should say no. Number one, Rob was not a believer. Number two, Dad's rules for dating had not changed. And number three, even though I liked Rob's laugh, he was certainly nothing like my ideal date. Not like Justin.

"I'm sorry," I said. "I can't. Dad's rules. But if you want, you can join my friends and me at our table sometime."

"The Prayer Table," he said.

"Yeah. Would that hurt your reputation, sitting with us Prayer People?"

"Maybe if I were a jock type. But my guys don't care. They're big on tolerance." He tugged my book bag strap. "See you tomorrow."

"See you."

I headed for my next class, feeling slightly depressed now that Rob's big grin and broad shoulders were behind me. Eric's face floated in my mind. I found myself glancing at people's faces, looking for him—looking for some sign of the bad vibes Rob had mentioned.

I felt better once I had settled into my seat in social studies. Social studies was probably my quietest class because Mrs. Mawley, in spite of her passion for history, had a very soft, pleasant voice, and about half the class usually fell asleep before the period was over.

Besides Haley and Savannah, two other students were missing today. Probably out with the flu. The blinds on the windows were closed against the afternoon sun, which was warm in spite of the chill air outside. I felt myself growing drowsy as Mrs. Mawley's voice rippled on and on.

I tried to keep myself awake by doodling flowers in my notebook.

*So much for Rob's vibes,* I told myself. *Too bad. I wish something interesting would happen.*

I glanced at the clock. Twenty minutes left till the bell.

Nineteen.

And then Todd Kendall stood up and pointed a gun at Mrs. Mawley.

# 23

## Haley

### In Haley Fields's Bedroom

Haley lay in bed, her long blond hair loosely braided and fastened at the end with a pink elastic. She had been throwing up every hour for the past five hours, and she wanted to keep her hair as clean as humanly possible. The whole stomach flu thing made her feel like a kid again—and not in a good way. It apparently reminded her mom of Haley's childhood too; she had taken the day off from work and popped into the bedroom every half hour to insist that Haley "drink fluids to stay hydrated."

Haley was watching TV through half-closed lids, wondering where the reporters dug up some of their disgusting new stories.

"We pause for breaking news from Mourning, Vermont. There is a developing hostage situation at the local high school. Apparently one or more students are holding a teacher and a classroom full of their peers at gunpoint. No names are being released, and we have no further details at this time."

"Mom!" Haley screamed.

She heard her mother coming down the hall, hurriedly ending a phone conversation, but she heard none of the actual words. Her eyes and ears and mind were focused on the TV. The newscaster was speaking to some expert in a suit about school violence.

Her mother stepped through the door and glanced at the TV screen, with the image of Mourning High in the upper right corner. "Oh, no."

She turned off the TV, took the remote from Haley's bedside table, and put it on the dresser. "Honey, I'm sorry you had to hear about it like that. I just got a call from Mrs. Truman. Thank the Lord you stayed home today."

"Liam?" Haley whispered.

"He's okay. He's in the elementary school building. I'm going down there to pick him up." Her mom laid a hand on Haley's arm. "Honey, you have to stay here, okay? Be brave, just for a little while till I get back. And don't watch the news."

"Mom!" Haley nearly choked on the word. "I'm not ten years old, okay?"

"Right. You'll be fine. Okay, I'll call you when I get there."

She left the room. Haley listened until the front door closed and her mother's car started. Then she climbed out of bed, fighting the nausea that rolled through her stomach, and seized the remote.

The news station was showing footage of the outside of Mourning High School, while a reporter rattled on about the email threats and police investigations. The parking lot of the school and the street in front of it were jammed with police cars and a half-dozen other emergency response vehicles.

"Most of the people in the building have been evacuated safely. The situation seems to be confined to a single classroom on the west side of the building."

*West side? Where would Nikki be at this hour? Social studies with Mrs. Mawley. That room was on the west side.*

"Oh dear God," Haley whispered. "Keep her safe. Please, please—oh!"

Her stomach rebelled, and she ran to the hall bathroom to throw up. When it was over, she came back and lay down in bed.

*Thank the Lord you stayed home today.*

# The Silent

Her mother's words rang in her head. But how could she be thankful when she felt so guilty? What right did she have to be spared from what her classmates were going through—what Nikki was going through?

*Why me? There's nothing special about me.*

*And why them? They're not bad kids. They don't deserve this!*

*Who could do something like this?*

*What can I do? I have to do something!*

All questions, no answers. She closed her eyes to the footage of her school on the TV and prayed.

*God, please protect them. Bring them out of there safely.*

That detective had been right. There was a Silent—someone so good at pretending that no one saw his rage until it was too late.

*God, it's never too late for You. You're always right on time. At least, that's what Mr. Berkell says.*

*Please show me now. Show me that You're never too late.*

*Please.*

She prayed, and watched the TV, and prayed some more. It was so depressing to be all by herself in the empty house, praying alone.

*But I don't have to pray alone.*

She grabbed her phone from the nightstand. Thank goodness she had put Mrs. Berkell's and Mrs. Land's phone numbers into her contact list! She called Mrs. Berkell first. Her call went directly to voicemail.

"Hi, Mrs. Berkell," said Haley. She took a deep breath to steady her voice. "Um, I don't know if you've heard about Mourning High, but . . . there are people with guns in there, and they're holding some students. I think Nikki might be one of them. So . . . please pray. And tell everyone you know to pray too."

She snapped the phone shut and lay down again. A tear slid out of the corner of her eye, down her temple, and into her hair. She rubbed it away and blinked until she could see her cell phone screen clearly. Then she called Mrs. Land.

"Hello?"

"Hi Mrs. Land, it's Haley, from church."

"Haley! Hi, Honey! How are you?"

"Not good, actually," said Haley. "Have you been watching the news on TV, Mrs. Land?"

"I'll turn it on right now, Dear."

"It's my high school. There are kids with guns inside."

"Honey, are you at school now?" Mrs. Land's voice was tense.

"No, I'm at home."

"Thank the Lord. How about Justin and Nikki?"

"Justin was leaving after lunch today to go with his parents to Baltimore. You know his dad is looking for a job there. But Nikki—" Haley felt her face crumpling with grief. She pressed her hand over her mouth to stifle the sobs.

"Okay, Honey. Okay. I understand. Let's pray for Nikki. Let's pray for her right now."

# 24

## No Eyes Here

---

**Nikki's Digital Diary**
<Continued from Monday, November 7, 5:25 p.m.>

---

I can remember everything about that day as if it just happened.
I know that the memory will fade with time, but I can't imagine
that I will ever forget what I felt then. At first there was blank white
shock—the refusal of my mind to process what I was seeing.

---

Todd didn't shout. He didn't say anything. He just stood there,
holding the gun on Mrs. Mawley.

*This is not happening. This can't be real. I must have fallen
asleep in class, and I'm dreaming.*

The next minute, one of the junior boys walked into the classroom. It was Will, one of the boys I ate lunch with at Soza's—the
one whose girlfriend had broken up with him by text message. My
first instinct was to warn him, until I saw that he had a gun too.

He closed the door and pointed his gun at Larry in the front row.

"Get some paper and some tape, and cover the window," he
said. "Now."

"Easy, man," said Larry. I could see his hands shaking as he
tore sheets from his notebook. "I don't have any tape."

"Who has tape?" said Will.

"I have some in my desk," said Mrs. Mawley in a small voice. She reached inside the desk and held it up. The second boy snatched it and tossed it to Larry.

"Do it."

Larry taped the paper over the window in the door.

Suddenly Will's eyes met mine. For a second I thought he might say hello. And I thought how strange that would be.

But his eyes clouded with anger. "Stop staring!"

He pointed the gun at me. The instant he did, Larry yanked open the classroom door and bolted out. Will shot at him twice, and Angie began to scream. The door swung shut.

"Did you get him?" asked Todd.

"No," said Will. He shook his gun at Angie. "Stop that! Stop it now!"

She collapsed onto her desk, shivering with sobs.

"Will, you watch the door," said Todd. "Don't get distracted again. I'll handle the rest. Mawley, leave your desk and walk towards me."

Mrs. Mawley's face was white and her lips trembled. I had never seen such terror in a human face before. She moved towards Todd, foot by foot.

"Stop," he said. "Will, sit in Mawley's chair and watch the door. The rest of you, line up along the back wall."

Angie was still sobbing helplessly in her seat, so I took her arm and walked her to the back wall. I felt sick and shaky inside, as though my organs and nerves had suddenly turned to jelly. I couldn't think. My brain had frozen while trying to process what was happening.

We all stood shoulder to shoulder with our backs to the wall. I was conscious of raw, blind fear creeping through my mind. In a moment it would overtake my last shred of will and turn me into a screaming, hysterical mess.

*No,* I told myself. *No. Get a grip. God, help me get a grip.*

# The Silent

I took a deep breath and focused on the fake wood grain of the nearest desk, allowing everything else in the room to blur.

How should a Christian react in this situation? Should I try to witness to my classmates? Should I pray aloud, or sing a hymn?

*You can get through this. Just be quiet; don't antagonize them.*

Maybe it wasn't the voice of God, but it sounded like good advice to me, so I pushed aside any fleeting dreams of myself as a "hero of the faith." I had once heard a hero defined as "someone who gets other people killed."

For a while Todd sat backwards in one of the desk chairs and stared at us. After a while he got up and walked along the line, inspecting our faces. When he came to Angie and saw that she was still crying, he paused.

"Are you afraid?" he asked.

She was crying so hard she couldn't answer. He smacked the side of her face with his free hand and continued along the line to me.

"You don't seem scared," he said. "Are you?"

Was I? The jelly-nerves feeling was gone, and in its place was a kind of stony calm.

"I don't know," I said.

Todd held the gun inches from my face. "Are you scared now?"

There is nothing like the sensation of being a second away from death. The air buzzed in my ears, and I could feel every little current of air, see every fiber of Todd's T-shirt. The most basic instinct in the human race—the desire for survival—twisted up into my throat, choking me with the fear of death.

"Yes," I whispered. "Now I'm scared."

"Todd," said Will. "Somebody's coming."

Someone rapped on the classroom door. "Hello, Will. May I come in?" said a smooth female voice.

"Don't touch the door!" said Will. "I'll shoot."

"This is Stella Chandler of the Mourning Police. I just want to talk to you, Will."

"I'm not talking. Go away or we'll shoot them!"

"Could I speak to Todd?" said the voice.

Todd swore.

"Get away from the door!" Will screamed.

There was silence for a moment.

"I'll be back later," said the voice. "We'll talk then. I just want to help this end well for everybody."

I glanced down the line of students. Mrs. Mawley was at the end, looking as if she might faint any second. For my part, I felt as if I had stepped into the middle of a nightmare.

I had watched enough movies to know that the police were probably scurrying around like mad ants, making phone calls and reassuring parents and consulting with experts, trying to figure out how to get everyone out of the classroom alive. That would be complicated, especially since the room had only one door. And the resources in Mourning were severely limited.

I pictured a SWAT response team in black suits crashing through the ceiling to save us. That would mean gunfire and shouting, and an end to the situation—but not necessarily a happy ending. The police didn't know what was going on in the classroom, how we were all lined up execution-style against the wall. All they knew was what Will had told them.

In my imagination, I could hear the police on their radios. *"We have no eyes in the classroom."*

No eyes here where we were all about to die.

*Get a grip,* I told myself again. *Be positive. God won't let anyone kill you till it's your time to go.*

I had heard Mrs. Berkell say that once. Somehow it wasn't very comforting. What if it was my time to go now—today? Would it hurt much? If it hadn't been for that negotiator woman at the door, Todd might have pulled the trigger and blown my face apart. Surely that would hurt. Or maybe it would be like falling off a bike and scraping your knee; for a few seconds there's no pain, and then the stinging starts. Maybe being shot would be like that—numbness at first, and then maybe I'd be dead before the pain set in.

# The Silent

*How morbid, Nikki,* I told myself. *You're going to scare your-self stupid. Stop it.*

Todd and Will were just standing around, Will by the door, and Todd towards the back of the room where he could keep us covered with the gun. I wasn't sure which one of them to fear the most. Will with his nerves and his spastic trigger finger would probably shoot someone if startled, but Todd seemed more likely to shoot someone on purpose.

"Will? Todd?"

The voice at the door startled us all.

"Shut up!" yelled Will.

"We're willing to work with you here, but you have to tell us what you want, Will," said the negotiator.

"Tell her to back away, or else," said Todd.

"Back away from the door!" said Will. "Or I'll shoot you!"

"Will, we can still fix this," said the voice. "You haven't hurt anyone yet. We can still work this out."

I wondered how the negotiator knew that Will hadn't hurt any-one. Or was she guessing? And why wasn't she talking to Todd?

Will glanced at Todd, then back to the door.

*Keep talking,* I begged silently. *He's wavering.*

"We called your grandfather, Will," said the voice. "He wants to talk to you."

"Oh, no." Will pressed his fist to his forehead.

"He's going to call your cell phone. Is that okay?"

Todd shook his head.

"No," said Will. "Stop talking to me."

For several minutes there was silence. Then we all heard a loud buzzing from Will's pocket.

"Don't answer it," said Todd.

But Will reached for the phone.

"I said, don't answer it!" Todd sprinted to the front of the room. "Give it to me!"

He grabbed for the phone, but Will held it just out of reach. Todd lunged forward and gripped Will's wrist, twisting it until the other boy yelled with pain.

Some of the boys in our line looked at each other, as if they were wondering whether or not to charge.

"Don't!" I whispered.

They glanced at me, frowning. I shook my head, praying that they wouldn't try anything. By the time they got halfway across the classroom, Will or Todd would notice and shoot them.

Then the tussle was over, and Todd threw the phone onto the floor and shot a hole through it. Angie screamed.

Todd gripped Will's shoulder.

"Steady, man," he said. "They're messing with your head, trying to make you weak. Remember the plan, okay? Don't change the plan."

Will nodded.

The negotiator's voice came faintly through the door again. "Will, what happened? Is everything okay?"

"Tell them you killed Angie," said Todd, so low I could barely hear the words. "She was making you nervous. And if they talk to you again, you'll kill someone else."

"But—"

"Tell them!"

Will raised his voice. "I killed Angie! She was getting on my nerves. Don't talk to me again, or I'll shoot somebody else."

We all listened, waited for a response. When none came, Todd laughed.

"Now they think you've hurt someone," he said. "No more leniency for you, Will. They don't really care about you. They care about these robots." He gestured at the lineup of students. "Anyone who is different is a threat to them."

"Why are you doing this?" I said. "What do you want?"

"Shut up!" bellowed Todd. He strode toward me and stopped when his face was barely an inch from mine. His breath was hot on my face. I pressed myself back against the wall.

# The Silent

"What does anybody want?" he whispered. "To be special? To live forever? To die?"

I stared at him, confused. He was crazy. Of course he had to be crazy, to do something so terrible.

Did he know that there was no future left for him after this? Just a jail cell and a ruined reputation? No one would hire him, or marry him. No child would be proud to call him their father. Had he thought through all that before acting out? Probably not.

Or maybe he had. And maybe he intended to kill himself when he was through with us. People often did that, once they realized how far they had let themselves go. I had heard it on the news a dozen times.

"How is this going to end?" I whispered.

"I would have thought you'd understand," he said. "You're different too—like me." He pointed at the door. "They don't like anyone who is different. They want to eliminate us, trample us down and crush us into little pieces. Well, I'm not going to live in their world any longer. I'm moving on."

He backed away from me, still holding the gun ready. From the bag under his desk he took a package of black masks, the kind that covers your whole face. He tossed the bag to one of the boys. "Open it," he said. "Everybody put one on."

Angie started crying again, and two other girls joined her. They knew, as I did, that the masks were not a good sign.

"Let's get this party started," said Todd.

# 25

## The Myth of the Happy Ending

### Nikki's Digital Diary
<Continued from Monday, November 7, 9:18 p.m.>

---

I had to stop writing for a while. I had what Kaye calls a flashback—something worse than just a memory. I'm over it now, I think, though I can still see Todd, handing us each one of those black masks.

---

No one put the masks on at first; it was like accepting a ticket to see Death, up close and personal. We all stood there, holding our masks in our hands. Then Todd put his gun against Mrs. Mawley's head.

"Do it," he said. "Put them on."

I set my mask against my face and pulled the string over my head till it rested above my ears. One by one, my classmates obeyed too. Mrs. Mawley was no one's favorite teacher, but none of us wanted to see her die.

Through the eyeholes of my mask, I watched my fellow students. Instead of the faces I knew, I saw blank, dark ovals, each with the same round eyes and the same straight mouth. It frightened me more than the guns because I understood what Todd was doing. He was blotting out our personalities, turning us into the cookie-cutter creatures he thought we were. He was making it easier to kill us.

There must be something I could do to make this stop, something I could say to him to make him see reason.

"Todd," said Will. He was slumped in Mrs. Mawley's chair. "I don't think I want to do this."

"Hey!" said Todd. "Don't back out on me now, man. All you have to do is watch the door. Just watch the door. I'll take care of the rest."

Will pulled up the hem of his T-shirt to wipe sweat from his face.

"You don't have to listen to him, Will," I said before I could stop myself.

I saw Todd's fist coming and braced myself as it slammed into my right cheekbone. Pain seared through my face.

"One more word—just one—and I'll shoot you," said Todd. "That's a promise. Okay?"

I nodded. Tears were running from my eyes under the mask. I didn't dare lift it to touch my cheek. Was it bleeding or just bruised?

Over Todd's shoulder, I saw Will pick up the gun and point it at Todd. "I want out," he said. "I only did this to show Kayley."

*Show her what?* I wondered. *That you're a crazy idiot following a homicidal nut case? That's not the way to win back your girlfriend.*

Todd turned toward his partner, but kept his gun pointed at me. "You're not leaving."

*Shoot him, Will,* I thought. Then I realized that a shot at Todd would probably result in Will shooting me.

And then I realized that Todd's weapon was inches from my face, well within reach—and his head was turned away so he could watch Will. If I moved fast enough, maybe I could disarm him.

At this point I didn't have much to lose. Todd was obviously planning to kill us. Now was the time to act.

*Help me, God,* I prayed.

Todd had the gun in his left hand, so I sidestepped to the right, caught his arm in both hands, and pulled down as hard as I could. The gun went off, splintering the white plaster of the wall.

"Help me!" I shrieked.

Nick Rumminger tackled Todd from the back. I twisted Todd's left wrist, trying to make him let go of the gun. It went off again, and this time someone screamed, not in fear, but in pain.

Two more boys joined the struggle, and together we forced Todd to the floor. Nick stamped on his wrist and then kicked the gun away from his hand.

"Hold him!" I yelled. Then I looked for Will.

Will stood by Mrs. Mawley's desk, still holding the second gun. I had been counting on the fact that he wouldn't shoot, that he really wanted out of the situation. But the panic on his face told me that he was still a danger. If any of the boys tried to charge him or tackle him, he might still shoot.

I took a step toward him, my hands up. "It's over, Will. You can put it down now."

"Are they going to put me in jail?" His voice shook.

"I don't know," I said. "You didn't hurt anyone, so maybe not."

"You're lying!" he said. "They're going to put me in jail. I don't want to go to jail."

"The best thing you can do now is put the gun down," I said. "If you hurt someone, it'll make things worse. Please."

"Come on, man," said Nick. "Just give her the gun. It'll be fine."

I took another step toward Will.

Suddenly the classroom door opened and two policemen stepped into the room. Startled, Will turned toward them and shot. His bullet caught the first policeman in the chest.

I screamed.

Will kept shooting. I dove under the nearest desk and covered my head, chanting some kind of incoherent prayer—asking to live. My ears roared with the shots and the screaming and the yelling.

Eventually I realized that the noise had ended, and I stopped my feverish praying.

In the room I heard groans, and voices, and the shuffling of feet. I stayed under the desk until someone touched my arm and said, "Miss, it's okay. Everything's under control now."

I looked into the beefy face and kind eyes of a police officer. He helped me crawl out from under the desk.

The policeman who had been shot was alive; I could see him propped against the wall, talking to a medic. Apparently he had been wearing body armor.

"Anyone else hurt?" I asked.

"A couple of the students have injuries. Nothing fatal," he said. "Are you okay?"

"I think so."

"Let's have someone take a look at you, just to be sure."

As he led me out of the room, we passed Will. They were loading him onto a stretcher. His right forearm was covered in blood and bandages.

"You shot him?" I asked.

"To keep him from shooting anyone else," said the policeman.

"Thank you," I said.

In the hall I saw Todd being led away by two more policemen. Detective Daulton was in the hall, speaking with a dark-skinned woman whose voice sounded like the one that had spoken with Will through the door.

Kaye broke off her conversation and approached the officer who was with me.

"Have you found Nikki Altemann yet?" she asked.

I waved. "It's me."

"Nikki! I didn't recognize you. You have the—" She pointed to my face.

"Oh." I tried to pull the mask off, but it stuck to the right side of my face. "Ow!"

When I finally worked it loose and pulled it off, Kaye gasped. "You're hurt!"

I touched my cheek and felt the stickiness of drying blood. "Todd hit me."

"Come on, let's get you to the medics," she said, putting an arm around my shoulders.

"It's not like I'm dying," I said.

"Whatever. Come on."

The hallway was clogged with police officers and medical personnel, so I lowered my voice to a whisper. "I'm sorry."

"For what?" She looked surprised.

"I failed. I was supposed to figure out who might do something like this. And I didn't."

She squeezed my shoulders, and for some reason it hurt. Maybe I had banged my shoulder when I dove under the desk.

"You didn't fail. You did exactly what I asked you to do. You kept your ears and eyes open. But it was never your job to prevent this, only to provide a clue if it came your way. If anyone failed, I did."

"No one was killed," I said.

"From what the other kids have said, that was mostly due to your quick thinking."

I shook my head. "It was a stupid thing to do, but I figured at that point I didn't have a choice. He would have killed us. I know it."

Kaye sat with me while the paramedics checked me for wounds and cleaned up my face. When they had finished, she said, "We've been keeping the parents and the media outside for their safety, but I think it's time for you to see your family now. They're probably worried sick. Just don't talk to the reporters, okay? We'll tell them what they need to know. I'll come along to keep them off your back."

"Okay," I said. At that moment I wanted nothing more than to get out of that school.

When I stepped out into the sunlight, I felt like a completely different person from the one who had gone to school that morning.

# The Silent

I looked at the setting sun, at the flaming orange clouds around it, and I thought about how close I came to never seeing the end of the day. It turned me so weak that I could barely stagger across the lawn.

"Nikki! Baby!" My mother was hugging me, crushing me close to her. "You're okay, you're okay! We were . . . we were all so . . . I'm just . . ."

She burst into tears, and I patted her back, comforting her. I would probably need trauma treatment later, but for now, she was the helpless one.

When her sobs quieted, I moved on to the two people that I most wanted to see—my dad and my brother.

Dad hugged me and whispered, "I asked God to keep you safe, and He did."

"Yeah, I'm kinda glad about that too." Tears filled my eyes, but I wrestled them back. I would cry later, when I was alone.

"I wanted to go in there and shoot those two for you," said Tae. "But they wouldn't let me."

I gave him the best smile I could manage. It must not have been very good, because he looked away, his jaw muscles working as though he might cry or explode. When he hugged me, I thought my ribs would crack.

"Ow!"

"Aw, you're tougher than that." He pushed me away and thrust his hands into his pockets, staring fiercely at the school.

Behind him and Dad I could see Mr. and Mrs. Berkell, and Mrs. Land, and Haley's father. And then, before I could find any other faces I knew, Justin's arms were around me.

He backed away almost instantly. "You're okay." His face was red, maybe from anxiety and maybe from the hug.

"Yeah," I said, my own face heating up.

"Haley's at home," he said.

I nodded. "She was sick."

A few weeks ago, a hug from him would have sent me to the stars. But now, I told myself, it was just good to know that he cared.

They all cared, every one of the people embracing and weeping on the school's lawn. Those among them that knew Christ had prayed for me and for my classmates.

And God listened.

---

In the stories or movies that I like best, there is a happy ending. All the twists and turns are straightened out, the lovers are reunited, and the bad guys are punished. Stuff like that.

Real life is totally different. I'm not saying that there are no happy endings—just that they are never perfect. Maybe that's why we like books and movies and stories so much, because it gives us a chance to make things work out like they should.

It wasn't a happy ending for Todd and Will, or for their families. And it wasn't a happy ending for the police either, since they had to explain to the media why they couldn't prevent the incident when they had been warned that it was coming.

Everyone keeps telling me to get rest. It's like they all expect me to be traumatized by what happened, and maybe I am. But the truth is, I feel like I've been asleep for a long time, and now I'm awake. I have lived more in the past month than in all my seventeen years so far.

I'm sitting here, in my room, looking at all the normal things that don't seem quite so normal anymore. I survived one of the most harrowing events that could happen to a teenager, or to anyone. And if I learned one thing, I learned that few people are what they seem to be. Only God knows a person's mind. And only He can heal the pain of a heart.

It's not a perfectly happy ending for me. The school year is not over. Justin is leaving. Tae isn't out of his own darkness yet. And my mother is still looking for the love that will make her happy.

But I'm not discouraged, because in this world, the end is never really the end.

It's just another beginning.